WILHELMINA: An Imagined Memoir

By R J McCarthy

Scuffletown Press

WILHELMINA: An Imagined Memoir

Copyright © 2014 by R J McCarthy

ISBN-13:
978-0692227954

ISBN-10:
0692227954

Printed in the United States of America
Scuffletown Press
Henderson, NC
First Edition
rjmccarthybooks.com
Cover photograph courtesy of Linda Rhodes Jones and Wilhelmena Rhodes Kelly, private collection.

For

Linda Rhodes Jones & Wilhelmena Rhodes Kelly
(Granddaughters of Wilhelmina Johnson Hamlin)

Leo Ostebo
Salvatore N. Misiano
The Kings Park Heritage Museum
The People of Kings Park

Susan Holly Spire
The Holton-Arms School
Class of 1961

Contents

WILHELMINA: An Imagined Memoir

Foreword

In October, 2012, the author returned to his high school for the first time in 44 years. While there, he visited a museum dedicated to the history of Kings Park, New York. Thanks to the efforts of a former teacher, Leo Ostebo, the museum he founded continues to flourish.

There were few black kids in the school when the author attended (class of 1960), none that he could see upon his return. Through Mr. Ostebo, he learned that an orphanage for black children had existed in Kings Park from 1911 until 1918, when it ended in tragic circumstances. Unaware of its existence, he stood astonished before a picture of the forgotten institution. He felt as if a page in a history book, in his education, had been omitted. It stirred something ineffable in him, a splinter beyond removal.

Learning of two living descendants of an orphanage "inmate," an idea began to taxi. It took flight upon meeting Linda Rhodes Jones and Wilhelmena Rhodes Kelly, granddaughters of the inmate, Wilhelmina Johnson Hamlin. They generously took time to share with him the scant details of their grandmother's too-short life. What permeated the mossed-over past was a feeling that "Wilhelmina" was loved by those in possession of those fragmented details.

He had stumbled upon one of those unknown millions who has contributed more to the furtherance of *humanity* in the human race than a majority of the well-known ever will. In a very short time on this planet, she created a legacy of love.

Now in full writer's flight, he decided that, in order to recognize the worth of her life, he had to assemble an armature based on those few verifiable facts. Animating the framework, to bring Wilhelmina Johnson Hamlin to life, became the quest of his imagination.

WILHELMINA: An Imagined Memoir

Wilhelmina Johnson Hamlin

1903-1930

Chapter One: Strange Math

I was never an "orphan." *Never*. No matter what someone might say or the word might imply. Yes, for a time I lived in an orphanage, The Howard Colored Orphanage. Established in Brooklyn, it later relocated to Kings Park, New York as the Howard Orphanage and Industrial School. But *I* was not an orphan.

Please, do not misunderstand. I am not speaking ill of orphans, implying they were less than me. Could not be farther from the truth. But I had parents, that's right, two of them all the time I was in the orphanage.

I never fully understood why I and my little brother, John Henry, were placed in the orphanage. But I have no doubt it was about money. Our parents both worked, struggling to survive on not enough.

I am good with numbers, always was. But I have seen some strange math in my life, things that refused to add up. Have you ever seen $1 + 1 = 0$? Or even less than? I have. My parents were proof of this math not taught in schools. Two people working for too little.

My mother, widowed when she married my father, brought two surviving children (of twelve) into the marriage. By the time John Henry and I came along, there was little available for colored children. Orphans or victims of poverty, it did not matter. Boarding schools? If you think about that long enough, you might get a laugh. No? Okay, probably not. But you have to look for laughter whenever you can and wherever you can find it. And songs. And sunlight. Stir them together, yeast the mix with love, and *presto*. Magic!

Math? Alchemy? Turning slag into gold? Whatever it was, you might come up with something good, and that was okay with me.

Yes, my father, William, was a man of color. I do not know it as a fact, but I always suspected I was named after him. "Wilhelmina" was probably as close as they could get. Fact or no, it does not matter. I like to think of it that way. In time, I was nicknamed "Bill."

More odd math. Have you seen $1 + 1 = 1$? I have. Every child of a mixed-race marriage has. And those children are proof of this math, also not taught in schools. I learned that the child of a colored parent and a white parent is always "colored," never "white." How does that work out? I am kidding. I know. It was just a chance to laugh. If I did not, who knows what might come out. As I said, I prefer to laugh. And sing. And find a corner of sunlight.

At the orphanage, we were referred to as "inmates." It was not an unkind place, but you would hear the word when adults talked about us as a group. *Inmates*. It brought to mind *prisoners*.

Strange, how the words you choose can sometimes lift you up or pound you into the mud. That is a truth for me, something I have noticed all my life. Depending on how you say them, there are not many neutral words in this world. Not in English, anyhow. I suspect that is true for all languages.

It is up to us to neutralize those words. Laugh when you hear them. Take to singing or turn to the sun. colored people know all about that, know it as children.

I suppose I might have thought of the orphanage as some kind of boarding school. For me, no matter how long I was there, it was always temporary. Like going to camp, which I never did. Or going to college, which I never did. Or taking a vacation. A vacation? That was just a word, a word that expressed distance and "other," kind of like a fairy tale.

Words again. Can you tell they are important to me? I am smiling. Of course they are. I just said so, did I not? Words were a map for me. Not just what I could or could not say, they warned me where I could go or not. They often signified like a blinking red light at a railroad crossing. Caution! Watch what you say! Careful now!

But being careful – "cautious" if you like – was not difficult for me. I believe it was my attitude. I had the right attitude for what came to me or what I was taken to. My mind seemed to move like an ice-skater, gliding through whatever I was doing rather than bumping against things.

Looking back, one might say I was adaptable, could adjust to what life presented. I do not take any credit for that. I did not set out to do it this way or that. It was just in me.

Maybe being a girl helped. Boys? So many of them seemed like a wind-up toy. When you let it go, it skitters all over the floor. No reason and no direction. Too many of them seemed willing to do anything to stay out of their minds. But for me, it was sanctuary, a private sunspot no matter how dark the day. While they often slept to escape the day, I wanted every minute of it.

I was happy, way more than I was not. At home, in the orphanage, later in school (PS 28 in Brooklyn), it did not matter. I could find a way to be happy. Set me a task some saw as drudgery, I would sing, out loud if possible, in my heart if not. If drudgery was a gloomy Gus with grasping hands, I was a greased pig.

I loved to sing. You have probably guessed that by now, many times as I have already mentioned it. I was good at it, probably because I loved it. Had "range and good tonal quality" according to Reverend Gordon, superintendent of the orphanage.

There I was, part of an all-girl singing group, "The Quartette." We performed in these beautiful dresses, white as dogwood blossoms. Not so secretly, I knew we were part of endless fund-raising at the orphanage.

"See those beautiful colored girls in their pure white dresses, their voices angelic. This is what your donations go for."

Did not matter. I loved to sing. And the money was badly needed, so that was fine with me.

Again, money. Though a blot on my life, it would not determine who I was.

From it all, I emerged with a treasured life. So many around me died young, death as often tragic as it is natural. I would like to tell more about it. There is so much there that when I speak of the orphanage, I am focusing mostly on 1915. I turned twelve then, a time of vast change. I went from a child's world to a new world I had to learn all over again.

Returning to 1915 (I am now twenty-six), I was scarcely aware of the happenings at that time. Historical happenings. My goodness, a war was going on in Europe, one that America ended up in. But up close, through the eyes of a twelve-year-old, my tiny world was full.

Chapter Two: Magic or Mirage?

Can something be magical and not, at the same time? If it can, it would be Kings Park.

By 1915, I had been in The Howard, on and off, for about eight years – mostly on. In 1911, the orphanage moved from Brooklyn to *the country*, the town of Kings Park, fifty miles east on Long Island.

We did not know it at the time, but we were part of a test of sorts. Some well-meaning people were attempting to bring Booker Washington's ideas about educating colored children to the North. "Tuskegee North" someone called it.

There had been a battle of ideas between Mr. Washington and another man, W.E.B. DuBois, about how to best carry this out. It seemed to me they came at it from different directions. Mr. DuBois, you might say, preferred to work from the top down. He wanted to go after the minds of colored children, educating them to the highest.

Mr. Washington, on the other hand, wanted to work from the ground up. A more practical man some said, he felt an education of ideas would not best serve the colored race. He felt we needed a more basic education, directing us to the "Industrial Arts." It was his belief we could "bootstrap" ourselves by our skills, proving our worth to the White race.

Privately, I used to wonder how I would prove one half of myself to the other. Once, while I was thinking this, someone asked me why I was smiling. I said, "I don't know." But I did. To no one's surprise (at least not mine) Mr. Washington's ideas won support. I believe they were less scary to white people. Heavens to Betsy, colored people with ideas! It is still funny, if you let it be. I did, and I do. It helps me. Otherwise, I might be thinking about that all the time rather than living my life.

They wanted to bring us along "gradually," *slowly*, to my way of thinking. Make the boys carpenters, shoemakers, farmers and such; the girls domestics. It would prepare us for adulthood, give us a way to earn a living. I believe it was well-intentioned. But I also believe we would be the labor for rich people. No one ever said that to me. It just came to me years later, floating in like a breeze carrying the smell of warm bread. Or a distant moan. Suddenly, you know what it is, don't need anyone else to tell you.

That was okay, I guess. Labor is honest, real, you can see the results, touch them. But it can also be hard, sometimes makes for a hard life. And that is enough about that for now.

I was speaking of *magic*. The magic was Kings Park. You take city-bred kids (though some were from Virginia and South Carolina) and drop them in the country? Going to sleep in tight city streets, buildings standing shoulder to shoulder with their shadows. And, *presto*, waking up in fields blessed with blue-sky sunlight. *Magic!*

Rather than being asked to leave The Garden of Eden, it was more like being invited in. The Howard Orphanage and Industrial School was plunked down on a huge farm. There were horses in Brooklyn, usually pulling a cart. But there were also trolleys and motor cars, and you had to watch out for them. Hot, screeching things smelling of burning oil, scorched metal, and dried-up leather, they came on you faster than a working horse. It was like learning to live all over again, especially with those cars.

At The Howard, there were horses – and cows, pigs, chickens, too – but hardly ever a bleating motor car. The roads were little more than rolled dirt and hollowed ruts. A town man would come and scrape the orphanage road, hopelessly trying to smooth those axle-breaking ruts. Once they dried, those ruts were hard as concrete, harder even. The name of the road added to the magic. Indian Head. *Alacazam*! I am living in the Old West.

On a map, those roads were drawn straight as a soldier at attention. But when you saw one, twisty as licorice, it was as if a ribbon had floated down from above. It landed as Indian Head.

To travel beyond Kings Park, you rode the Long Island Rail Road, not a motor car. It was your only choice back to Brooklyn and New York City or …? There was no "or" for me. I knew no "or."

If the wind was blowing right, you could hear the train as it approached the station. Its hoarse, insistent horn warned: Do not be loitering on the tracks. The locomotives (we called them "steam engines") were both awe-inspiring and terrifying. They seemed to hiss, "I am so-o tired," as they bled oil and water.

Yet from a distance, the horn also sang "Hello," kind of like a town crier, on a clouded

evening, calling out "All is well." It was comforting.
"Right now, everything is normal. You are safe. Be
back tomorrow night, checking on you."

Can you hear the math? It is measurement, so
important in everything I do, make, or see. Up close
or far away, the same thing? Yes and no. Like the
horn, you know it is the same when you are right
under it or hearing it far off. But it does not feel the
same, not nearly. It is like two different things, one
monstrously loud, the other a lullaby cooing you to
sleep. The same set of numbers, two different
answers. Which is correct? I would say both.

That is why, when I try to remember
something, I not only look back from a safe distance
but try to dig in close to see if it comes out the same.
If it does, then it must be a true thing.

There I go again, wandering from "magic."
But not really. To a child, so much was new in Kings
Park; it had an abracadabra feeling at times.

It was also not magical. It was life, hard along
with the soft. Sometimes, it seemed as if there was
way more hard than soft. You were grateful for those
soft moments, but the hard could be really hard, and
not easily forgotten.

Winter on Long Island was harder than stone,
and colder. It was a time of wind, sweeping in off the
Atlantic Ocean or down from Long Island Sound. It
slashed and cut like a blade through wheat. It made
cold *colder*. It began around November, petered out
in April. You were so used to it, it was probably gone
a month before you knew it. Sometimes there was
snow, and things stayed iced up for a long time, but
there was always wind. There were times when I

imagined I was living somewhere out west, Nebraska maybe.

At The Howard, it was a time of not enough. Not enough coal for heating, not enough warm clothes. Not enough *shoes!* We depended on donations, and sometimes they trickled in like a stream in drought. Winter was, by far, the hardest time.

Spring, summer, autumn, we went barefoot. The kids from Virginia and the Carolinas? It was not a problem. They were used to it. But even for them, when winter came, the magic was gone.

You look at those old pictures from The Howard, the ones where we fancied up for the Trustees. You see us all dressed up, the girls in pinafores, the boys in jackets and knickers – all wearing shoes. Count up those you see in the picture. Math again. Well, there were 250 of us. The ones you did not see were not wearing dresses or jackets. And some were not wearing shoes.

Most of the time, we wore smocks, catch-as-catch-can, whatever we had, whatever had been donated. It was a grab bag of cast-offs. The good clothes – and shoes – were for pictures that said, "See how well we are doing. Your donations at work. Please keep them coming so we can keep up the good work. Nothing is too small."

There were never enough shoes, never mind good shoes. John Henry and I went home in 1915 so I never saw the worst. I believe I did see the best, and Thank Heaven, I was not there for the worst. That came early in 1918, mid-winter, when the coal ration never arrived. When the radiators froze, several children suffered from frostbite. At least two had their feet amputated. I was told the war effort took our coal. Maybe. *Maybe*. Horrible as that was to think about, I hope that was not the reason. I do know The Howard never recovered.

Chapter Three: A Closer Look

March 21st was not the first day of spring. That was the day I could shuck off my tired winter shoes, and go barefoot. Gone was the worn leather with cracks growing like branches, my feet no longer burning from the cold. When important white people in suits and gowns came to inspect us, the shoes went back on. Other than on special occasions, the shoes were forgotten until first frost. *That* was the day winter began, not December 21st or whatever day *The Farmer's Almanac* declared.

By my measure, spring usually arrived late, winter early. In between, my feet developed a shell of callus, rock-hard to bruising stones, stickers or insect bites. Housemothers dreaded the occasional splinter that found a way through that stiff crust. It was almost impossible to remove.

Spring arrived on an April Tuesday. I knew that, because it was ironing day. Monday wash, Tuesday iron. The difference between the days was the difference between a spider bite and a tick bite. You could argue about it, but why bother? Had anyone asked me, I would have held up two fingers, squeezing them less than an inch apart.

By necessity, every day at The Howard was a workday. Weekdays were training and school, half and half. While half the children attended school in the morning, the rest trained in the work they would be doing. Training was as much a part of the orphanage's functioning as it was to prepare the children for life beyond. While I trained in the "domestic arts," that training was put to use at The Howard. Inmate girls did the washing, ironing, sewing, much of the cooking, and almost all of the cleaning. The boys brought training in carpentry, farming, barbering, and shoe repair to their share of the orphanage's maintenance.

I preferred the shift that placed me in school during the mornings. I was wide awake then, my mind never fresher or more open, stretching to the lessons. The Howard provided us an eighth grade, New York State-approved, elementary education.

Almost twelve, I sensed the difference between "training" and "work" was narrower than the insect-bite comparisons. I accepted it, choosing to dig no deeper than the orphanage's need for shared work.

The work had its rewards as well. The constant tasks, and the concentration required, helped me not think so much about home and my parents. During school lessons, there were lulls when my mind drifted into daydreams ending at the doorway to loss. Then too, during the work, you could sing or hum, depending upon the housemother's mood that day.

One morning, feet planted on the varnished wood floor, I took an extra moment in front of the bathroom mirror. Face washed, teeth brushed, I arched up on my toes for a closer look, working a brush through tangled hair. "Busy hair," someone had called it; it was the gift of a mixed marriage.

Bountiful in the way of my mother, it ribbed and rucked with curl, my father's contribution. I had never suffered the pain some of the older girls went through to add length to their hair. Some of the Carolina girls called it "good hair."

Good hair? I thought. There was no way to laugh or sing my way to an easy peace with that. I had seen too many burned scalps. And the *smell*? Whew!

The boys did not do that, not that I could see. (Now, I even see men doing it.) I noticed things like that. At times, it seemed I noticed things other children did not or, at least, noticed less. Maybe it was that I wanted to remember them. What lay in people's minds behind the faces they presented to the world? It fired my thoughts, set them hungering for more knowledge.

John Henry's hair was more like our father's. More tightly curled, it combed out closer to his head and perfected his handsomeness. Why would a boy even want to subject himself to such agony? John Henry's hair was already *good*.

The thought of my brother reminded me I meant to check on him at breakfast. Like a prayer, it was a daily observance, a promise made to a tearful request from our mother.

"Keep an eye on him, won't you, lass?"

Simple, part of a painful good-bye, but my nod was a sworn oath cut in graveyard stone. I would have done it anyway, but the words became a connection to my mother, fingertip touching a fingertip. I believe my love of children began with my "maternal" concern and care for my brother.

I was still prodding my hair, poking at it, pushing it some here, tugging at it there. For some unknown reason – a mystery to be solved – I had begun to spend more time on my hair. Its care was more important than ever before. In fact, with increased mirror time, I had quietly started looking more closely at my face.

When I sang with "The Quartette," more than one adult had told me, "You look so pretty." I wondered how they knew that. Lovely to hear, I wondered what led them to say that.

Until then, "pretty" or "beautiful" arrived in pleasing voices, kind words, warm hearts. Not so much how people looked, it came from within. Beauty was my mother's brogue, my father's presence, the sudden jump-up of joy. It lay in the glorious red of Indian Head apples or a green field of alfalfa. Or it might be the shy scent hiding in a sprig of lily-of-the-valley. Where did I fit into this trove of wonder?

The face staring at me from the mirror refused to answer my curiosity. It was propped on a chin set firmly as a road sign. Just over it sat a broad mouth that widened easily into a white-toothed smile. In time, I would learn that others could see my spirit in that "generous" smile. A housemother once told me my cheekbones could "offer rest to a tired bird." When I looked at her, she added, "that's a compliment, child." Adding to the mirror's mystery, the large eyes of a watcher followed me through smoky-quartz-brown irises. And crowning it all, my "busy" hair. Despite all the brush strokes, to which I added a few more, the hair decided where it would go.

Time moved swiftly for me, more so it seemed than it did for most children. A full day, no small part of it, was not enough to account for it. It also had to do with what I brought to it, spirit and intention.

Breakfast a blur, I had carried only the scent of fresh-baked bread into the day. Smell anything baked, and everything would be okay. The morning's schooling had passed almost as quickly. My normal concentration, as fixed as a post, was wobbling. Several times uncalled memories of the mirror flashed by.

Later, ironing, I was freer to think about this growing curiosity in how I appeared to others. I could only absorb it in tiny spurts. Think about it too long, and it vanished, circling into confusion that left me light-headed. To avoid that, I would hum or break into song, a songbird praising life.

Usually, old camp songs meant to be sung in groups, burst forth. "She'll Be Comin Round The Mountain" or "I've Been Workin' On The Rail Road" were among my favorites. But this day, "Let Me Call You Sweetheart," a modern song, had threaded itself into the music. A more private song to me, its sentiments more personal, I hummed it at first. Without thinking, I lengthened my ironing strokes, timing them to the lilting march of the song. Gradually, the words worked their way with me, and the hum became a whispered melody.

"Let me call you sweetheart, I'm in love with you.

Let me hear you whisper that you love me

too."

When the words faded, a distant train disappearing, I would "da-da-da" a trestle across the forgotten lines.

Not exactly fond of ironing, I enjoyed the final product, stacks of folded bed-linens and clothes. I preferred the older, heated flatirons or mangles to the newer Steam and Dry Irons, filled with water. The latter afforded double the opportunity for harm, scalded by water or burned by the iron. With the flat iron, I could sprinkle water where it was needed, just ahead of my smoothing strokes. A sense of control was important to me, something I so rarely had, or so it seemed.

My thoughts began to flick toward the morning lesson and the current war in Europe. It was as if they had a mind of their own. The idea of war not only disturbed my waking hours, but my dreams as well. To ease away from the responsibility for something I could do nothing about, I began once more to hum. When my silent grief for the dead weighed too heavily, I switched to words.

"By the light …of the silvery moon…
I want to spoon…da-da-da-da-da da da da ..
Honeymoon…da-da-da-da-da da……"

Chapter Four: Indian Head

Four years earlier, when we trained from Brooklyn to Kings Park, the children thought we were going to heaven. In a way, it was, for city kids especially. In one day, we traveled from concrete and cobblestones to dirt roads and broad spaces. And the air? It was still September, but it was as if we had slipped through a curtain. From the stifling smells of Brooklyn - tar, metal, sunbaked stone – we stepped into a mild breeze that salted the tongue. Not far inland from Long Island Sound, you could sometimes smell the ocean at Indian Head. The only part that had not changed was the horse clods along the road.

It was an Eden as well for most of the children from the South. The adventure was the same for those from cities. Some of the country kids had known only the hole-in-the-stomach poverty of ramshackle sharecrop farms. Indian Head was a giant, above-the-clouds, step-up.

To behold the farm under a breeze-softened September sun was to gaze at a picture in a magazine. Fields, in the midst of harvesting wheat, corn, alfalfa, still green running to brown, yellow and gold. Fields, stretching to woods, dotted with a fish pond and islands of apple trees, chestnut trees and grape vines. The tiny orchards tossed their fruit, devil-may-care, to the ground. Enchanted children plucked at it like discovered treasure and stuffed themselves to bursting. Turtles sunned themselves on mossy rocks or water-smoothed branches poking above the pond. An occasional fish rippled the quiet water, letting you know it was really there.

In time, if we needed something and could grow it, we grew it. What we did not eat, we preserved. Apple butter. Pears, plums and peaches, huckleberries, too. Tomatoes and corn, beets and okra, cucumbers. Apple and grape jelly, pickles. We grew potatoes, cabbage, pumpkins, onions, beans. Wheat. Alfalfa for silage and fodder corn for the animals. We grew it all.

The sun coming down in the late afternoon, songbirds began to revive, filling the air with music. The chattering of excited children, once past awe, quickly overwhelmed the birdsong.

The centerpieces were the magnificent buildings: the cow barn, sprawling like a giant warehouse, but pleasant to look at; the dairy where the boys would separate the cream from the milk and churn our butter; the dignified farm house that would become Superintendent and Mrs. Gordon's home. Even the lowly chicken coops seemed fit for this postcard world.

And the cottages! The cottages where we would live, eat, sleep and learn. Cottage? When I heard the word in the past, I thought of something cozy, just right for a fairytale family. Set off a bit far from the farm buildings, these were large, two-story dormitories. Three, if you counted the attic. Newly built or freshened for our arrival, each had a recessed porch where I would sit when it rained. Sit and think. Dream. Think more about the future than the past, thinking the world I wanted into possibility – or trying to. Thinking when-my-ship-comes-in thoughts.

Since we did not have a school or chapel yet, one of the cottages served both needs. That kept our number down from the 300 they had planned to the 250 they had room for. Money, again. Always money. I do not allow myself to hate, but I do not like that word, *money*.

Back to words. Words have always been so important to me. I was always careful with them. I am teaching my children to be that way. It was about being colored in a white world, something we learned through tone of voice and sharpness of gesture. Sometimes, you received a sermon in a hard look.

But it was more than being colored, way more. It was about what was in me, about me being me. It was about understanding that once you say something, it stands like a statue, forever. You cannot erase it nor pretend you did not say it. And you cannot control how other people hear it.

Throw a stone in a pond, you cannot stop the ripples. So you have to be prepared to live with what you say. Somehow, I always knew that.

"But words once spoke can never be recall'd." Those are the words Reverend Gordon used one Sunday in chapel to open his sermon. I supposed they came from The Bible. It was as if I had already heard them, echoing from some private chamber in my mind. He went ahead and explained them, but he did not have to for me. I understood.

Years later, I found them in an old, cracked

leather copy of Bartlett's Familiar Quotations. A Roman, Horace, had spoken them more than 200 years before the birth of Christ. Wow! I thought. At the time, I could not find a copy of the book they originally appeared in, *Ars Poetica*. I cannot say I really looked that hard for the book because I already understood his words. I lived by them. You might even say, I *lived* them.

To say what you really want to say, you have to think about it first. And when you are upset about something, the first thing you want to do is say nothing. Not right away. You do, you might blurt out something you will regret. When you are upset, you cannot think. That is when terrible things get said, things that can hurt. Can maybe even damage.

I had to think first. I do not know whether it was always so or required of me. Whichever came first, chicken or the egg, I preferred to think. I secretly thought of it as my strength, part of it. When you heard me say something, I believed it. It was the truth, best I could tell.

I want my children to think, too. I want to teach them the difference between being careful with what you say and being modest. Careful is for someone uncertain, ill-at-ease, maybe even afraid. "Careful" is for someone else. I want them to understand that "modest" is for *you*. It is what you are, not what someone else says you have to be. Modesty is not showy but not afraid, either. To me, it means seemly, humble in your talents, proper. Free to be but not anything goes. Your strength is in what lies underneath. You are stronger than you appear. The strength is there, you know it. That is enough.

When I was twelve, a younger boy referred to a donor as a "fat old white lady." It was true, quite true in fact, but to say it where someone might hear it? There are some things, probably many, you can think that do not need to be said. It is about who you are, who you want to be. If I can teach that to my children, especially by example, I will have been a good mother.

Back to Indian Head Farm. When we first arrived, my senses almost drowned in the Thanksgiving table of colors, smells, the feel of the place. Did you ever touch the bark of a tree? Run your fingers over its skin? I have. Try it sometime. Touch a hickory, then maybe a maple or a birch. They are so different it will startle you, one nut hard and shaggy, the other smooth in places. It is as if they come from different worlds. After a while, I could close my eyes and know what I was touching.

And smells? A farm is a free-for-all of smells, some dry as dust, some so "sweet" they attack your nose. But almost all of them were good smells. Wheat chaff, horse sweat, starch. A potted gardenia. Oiled leather. A sun-dried table cloth. Planed wood. Anyone after a hot bath. The only smell I still take exception to – not the smell, what people say about it – is "sweet manure." I am not sure how those two words came together. Sweet? I would not say that.

Beyond the senses, it was a hard life. Not a bad life, but one with days filled with unending labor. It was a familiar life to the Southern children, and as I said earlier, better for most of them. But for city-bred kids, Southern or Northern, I was not so sure. As I understood it, the idea was to make some of the city kids into farmers. I wondered how that would be possible for colored boys who had known only city life. Now and then, I still wonder about that.

Hard as life was at The Howard, it was also like forbidden fruit, a temptation. I felt caught between what I hoped for (to go home) and the pull of Indian Head Farm. Have you heard of a push/pull problem? For me, it was pull/pull. If I let myself become too happy at The Howard, I was afraid I would lose remembrance of home. On the other hand, if I clutched too tightly to "home," would I become unhappy where I was?

One of my strengths was to find happiness wherever I was, but it was a never-ending battle.

Chapter Five: An Opportunity Lost

1915, my last year at The Howard. It was a Saturday, that I knew for sure, no matter how old the memory. The older boys were playing a baseball game against an outside team. That part of the memory fuzzes a bit, the other team either St. Johnland's or St. James's High School. The opponents were always white so that did not help.

My certainty the game took place on a Saturday was glued to an afternoon of freedom from duties. It could not have been any other day. Organized games on Sunday afternoons, following chapel services, were avoided, if not officially banned. Quieter freedoms were permitted for a few hours, fishing in Hog Pond, nature walks, small group play. Nothing loud and "rambunctious," as one of the housemothers used to say. It had to be Saturday.

While The Howard boys warmed up, I gathered with other students near the chalked lines to watch. I was wearing a faded blue, ankle-hugging dress and white pinafore, the usual. Please notice, I did not say "my" dress and pinafore. In my mind, it always was someone else's.

The boys were testing their arms, unleashing bolts of white lightning, trying to outdo each other before an audience. Catching those red-stitched balls produced yelps of pain, the amount bare hands could absorb. Few of them had even the raggediest of those flat-as-a-pancake mitts available in 1915.

It was the only time those hands touched new baseballs, just popped out gleaming from tissue-papered boxes. By game's end, those balls were lop-sided as soggy old socks filled with sawdust, and no longer white.

Just as I was casting about for a grassy spot to sit, an overthrown ball bounced off my ankle. I did not even have time to go "ouch!"

"Hey, li'l girl," one of the boys said. Hatless, his baby mustache proclaimed, *I am a man*, and rolled up, white sleeves, *I am a ballplayer*. Pointing to his other hand, he added, "Right here."

Several others yelled for me to return the ball. It was a rare day of freedom from chores for them, and they were bursting with it.

As if I had performed the act a thousand times, I picked up the ball and hefted it. With a snap of my arm, I let fly with a side-arm peg. The ball struck the intended palm with an astonishing *smack!* So hard, it made me nervous for a second.

"Dang!" went the big Virginian boy who had called for the ball.

Expecting a "powder-puff floater from a girl," as he later said, he dropped the "hot potato." For drama, he danced about and waved his hand as if it had been stung by a bee.

Several of the other boys doubled over in belly-grabbing laughter, yucking it up like myna birds. One or two slapped their knee in delight

"William can't catch a girl! William can't catch a girl!" filled the air, until Reverend Gordon hushed them. But whispers continued to trickle through. "William can't catch a little girl."

One of the boys closer to me said, "Say, you put some mustard on that chuck, Sis. How you do that?"

I thought he was a "Charles" from South Carolina, never knew for sure. His mustache was full. They preferred the boys to be clean shaven, but who was big enough to tell Charles?

I shrugged. I had never thrown a baseball before, knew only that it felt – familiar, felt right. Felt good. I had learned the sidearm motion skipping stones on the pond.

I remembered little of the game that followed. My thoughts had drifted to the different roads our lives were taking, boys and girls. I did not begrudge the boys their fun. But I found myself pondering a world that did not permit girls to play the game.

What was the choice for girls? I thought. Braiding a tether pole with ribbons?

Before my thoughts could further pick at the question, I was called away from the game. Along with some of the other girls, it was my turn to help prepare the Saturday evening meal.

I was by nature and necessity one who accepted life's whims. But I found my thoughts returning to the separations between boys and girls. Understanding escaped my mindful reach as I shucked ears of corn, peeled carrots and potatoes. Yet, I continued to think about who does what and the why of it. I was not questioning this way of the world so much as wondering about it.

I had once asked one of the housemothers why boys were directed one way, girls another?

Unable to recall what set off the question, I distinctly remembered the closing of the woman's face. An invisible curtain had fallen, hooding her eyes, flattening her face until it was unreadable.

After what seemed a measured silence, her voice almost sad, she said, "Because that's the way it is, child." And then she said nothing more.

My thoughts surrendered to corncob shelling and potato peeling, only to return later that evening. I would like to have tried baseball.

It couldn't be that hard, could it? I thought. I already knew I could throw it with "mustard." And the running part? I loved to run short races, even with all the clothes that got in the way. My little brother, John Henry, could scoot. So could I. We often played catch with a scuffed rubber handball or a worn-out tennis ball. Both were about the size of a baseball. Catching was not a problem for me, either.

The only part of the game unfamiliar to me was batting the ball. I was only too ready for that. Certain I could do it, it was never to be.

Twelve in 1915, I could already see certain freedoms coming to my brother and not to me. And here I was a year older than John Henry. Chief among them was choice. He could be a carpenter, shoe repairman, farmer, factory worker, mason, a trucker driving a team of horses. Maybe someday, a motorized truck. In fact, any field of labor I could think of was open to him. My choice was whether I offered my domestic skills for hire or within a family of my own. If there was another, I could not see it.

Secretly, this in itself was not a problem for me. Possibly, it was caring for my brother that unlocked a yearning in me for a family someday. It was the say-so in the matter, the choosing, that led me to pause. But, it was the loss of the joy of playing baseball that set off the questioning.

At twelve, the awareness of how we were steered could run just so deep, could only mean so much. My duties overtook curiosity before it became a throbbing ache I could not shake off like a staticky sock.

But the game had uncovered a gift, an ability denied with weak-tea reason. An ability that would remain an unopened gift, its potential and the joy to follow, unfulfilled. For that brief moment, I had stood in the light of recognition known only to boys.

Like the pain of childbirth, it would be quickly forgotten, only to return at the next delivery. Or whenever I happened upon boys playing baseball, and felt the twinge in my throwing arm, the twinge of an opportunity lost.

Chapter Six: My Secret Garden

There are places, and then there are *places*. Some you can see and touch, some private. A few you do not even suspect until something happens, and they pop out at you.

Most places can change. The place where you live can change in a heartbeat. Well, maybe not quite *that* fast, but almost. Miss a rent payment, and you will know. Night sound can change from trolley rumble and clatter to cricket chirps and the ghostly call of an owl. Or the hiss of summer silence.

I loved to hear the owl. Some of the Southern inmates were afraid of it, claimed it was a "haint" coming to get you. At least, that is what the older children told the younger.

"You hear that old owl calling?" Annie the Grump said to Little Alice, a five-year-old kindergartener. Annie loved watching the little ones curl up in wide-eyed wonderment and fear. "Means somebody's soul passing over tonight. Could be you."

She would make the owl sound and cackle like an old hen, the children vanishing under their covers. Little Alice just sat there, paralyzed.

When I heard an owl call, I felt as if someone were watching over me.

At The Howard, things were always changing. Seasons. You would go from the *green* green of spring to the golden brown of autumn, sometimes overnight it seemed. During the summer, you would go from early morning birdsong to a stillness at noon. Go from high blue sky to the coming down of purple-bellied storm clouds in just a few minutes. Go from bright this to dark that, sometimes in a finger snap. The other way round, it seemed to move slower. Why is that?

Same thing could happen with a private place in my heart. Not as easy, for sure not as quick, but it could happen. Sometimes, people you had feelings for might pull away, and you did not know why. Mostly, they just stayed away. They might give you a *why*, but it could sound hollow as a tunnel even as they said it. Kind of like they were trying to believe it even as they wanted you to. They would say, "On the up and up, I'll still be your friend."

What hurt the most was not the lie. It was that there was nothing I could say that would change it back. Someone was deciding for two people, but only one had any say. I cannot think of anything more unfair. Well, maybe I could, but right now I cannot.

The most important place for me, no matter what was happening, was the place in my mind. I held the only key to that door. If I wanted to let you in, you were in. But if I felt you would "disturb the peace," I put up an invisible "No Admission" sign. It flashed brightly in my mind, reminding me not to forget.

You might not even know. I would be polite; I was taught courtesy. Besides, it was not in me to hurt others, not even when I was upset. A housemother barking at you because her husband had yelled at her the night before. An older girl, struggling with her own changes, making fun of yours. A little child, missing his mother, slapping your hand away when you tried to comfort him. I just had no room in my mind for moody people. Could not let them pull me down like they do playing "King of the Hill." Sometimes, I was barely managing to hang on, too. My rope was frayed pretty thin.

The little child? I might try one more time, but if it was still, "No!" I respected his wishes. He would have to figure it out just like I did.

Kings Park, Indian Head Farm, the Howard Orphanage were places. So was Brooklyn, but my place was none of these. It was (still is) a place where whoever or whatever I loved could not be harmed. At The Howard, it contained my father, mother, and my brother, John Henry. Charter members.

That sounds funny, does it not? That is okay, I am laughing, too. Sounds like I needed a drop of humility added to a tablespoon of cod liver oil. They used to give it to us at breakfast. Yuck! I think it had something to do with Vitamin D for bone strength.

But that was the way it was at the time. I was as serious about it then as I was later when one of my children caught a cold. Without my permission, you could not be a part of my special place.

I believe my place in the mind saved me from giving up. It was amazingly powerful, like discovering a secret garden where you felt safe, and only you could find the door. (I loved that book, *The Secret Garden*.)

I would go there when something bad had happened. My parents could not come for a visit or someone having a bad day was mean to me. Maybe it was an older boy bullying John Henry. I tell him to "stop," and he then tries to bully me. I would just say "Goodbye," and go to my place in the mind. Mostly, I went there to think things out, to figure out what I could do, to make a plan.

To this day, I am a thinker more than a talker. Measured thoughts and care go into what I say. You may catch me sing-humming, but there is at least a tablespoon of thinking going on behind it.

I had to go to that place when John Henry and I were sent to the orphanage. In the beginning, I stayed there for a long time before I would dare peek out. It was even worse, *much* worse, when the orphanage moved to Kings Park. Most of the children were happy, as if they were to enter the Garden of Eden. But I was moving farther away from my parents.

"It'll be for the best, lass, you'll see," my mother said, through tears she could not hide. Or maybe it was my tears. But her face looked like a place where hard trolley tracks cross each other.

My father stayed away that day, Mama claiming he had to work. I think he could not bear to say, "Goodbye," and that is what I choose to believe.

Rather than the Garden of Eden, I slipped into my secret garden. Just like in the book, you had to squeeze through a hedge to find the door. Once inside, I settled into the place in my mind. Things there do not change. Well, not much and not easily. Everything remains in bloom regardless of season – blue delphiniums, pink climbing roses shinnying up a trellis, white phlox. My parents, my brother, they might age a bit, but they are there. And in it, there is laughter, singing. People smile a lot.

I had to have this place if I wanted to *visit* them. In Kings Park, my parents did not visit us much. More often, we visited them – which was not often. It was just too far from their work, so they said. Both of them worked, all the time it seemed, but I am not sure that was all of it.

I do not believe my father was comfortable traveling with my mother to a mostly white world. He could handle the looks, the whispers, the disapproving sighs people would make. "Tch! Tch!" or "Mm, Mm, Mm!" Add a shaking head, intention was clear.

I just think he was more comfortable staying in the colored world of Weeksville in Crown Heights, Brooklyn. It was only what I thought. He never said anything about it, and I never asked. If that was the way it was, why risk reminding him, leaving him uncomfortable just because I was curious. At the time, I doubted if I ever would ask him. I never did. He died in 1920, a month before I turned seventeen.

I wanted him happy when he saw or thought of me, to see himself in my eyes, in me. In my mind, he is.

In time, my garden grew with the entry of my husband and his family. His parents were good people, strict in their beliefs, but good. And of course, came my children, all five of them. A sixth on the way, I am due in March of 1930, less than five months from now.

My husband? My children? My world.

My husband, John F Hamlin, is a wonderful man, loving, his mind available to me when I need it.

Need him. I could not love him more.

My children? They are such good kids, all that I dreamed of, allowed myself to hope for. It is great fun doing little things for them – an ice cream in summer, a snow cone in winter. That is right, a snow cone in *winter*. Scoop some clear snow, pour a flavor over it, maybe some Carnation milk, and *Poof!* Magic! They respond so well.

And when they mess up – sooner or later they all do, what child does not? – they know. I do not have to yell, well, almost never. Dorothy, my third child, sensitive, more held in like I was, once dropped the baby after insisting on holding her.

"I can do it! I can do it!"

She could not, not that time. She was ashamed, her face frozen in horror. What more could I possibly have done to punish her? To look at her was enough. How would it have helped to yell at her? Besides, I needed to see to the baby, who was fine.

I do not go to my place in the mind, my secret garden, so much anymore. There is too much to do, so much to be happy about. I will still slip in from time to time when I need to think something through, no longer to escape. Now, the place I am in? I am where I want to be.

Chapter Seven: An Eye on John Henry

1915. It had been raining all morning, one of those drizzly Sundays where it was not going to stop. I did not mind. A serenity drifted down over me along with the rain, left me at peace with what was. Like a blanket placed around cold shoulders, it left me warm inside.

When it rained, the edges of my world might blur into mist, smudged like water paintings. But up close colors seemed to shimmer. They added a see-through clarity to my dreams, sleeping or awake. When the sun shone, glorious as it was, it tended to bleach those colors paler leaving them washed-out.

Chapel services complete, lunch clean-up finished, I decided to wander over to one of the boys' cottages. The rain was an opportunity to check on John Henry. I found him sitting on the top step of a covered porch, listening to one of the older boys. My brother and several other boys his age seemed spellbound, gathered around this near man. I eased into the corner of the top step, just out of the swirling rain, to listen. I was already a good listener, long before I knew it.

The boy, Ralph, was chewing on a toothpick, whittling another with a tiny penknife as he spoke. Beyond his age, long pants said he was a big-comb rooster in the pecking order at The Howard. John Henry and the other young boys sported knickers, most of them without knee stockings.

At eighteen, Ralph, a city-bred kid, was confident in all that he said. Besides, who among his young "altar boys" with their hanging mouths might challenge him? Ralph was nearing the end of his time at The Howard, knew they were having trouble placing him.

The staff thought he was not smart, that a lack of ability explained his failure to do better. They feared he would end up penniless, scuffling along the streets of the city. Sometimes, their worry darkened into disappointment as if they had taken his failure to thrive personally. They were unable to hide the anger he sparked in them, overlooking what they had tried to drive him to. More than a trade, his target was a return to New York City, to Brooklyn.

At the moment, he was the center of attraction and enjoying it. His eyes on his tiny carving, he was keenly aware of his worshipful audience.

"Farming?" I heard Ralph say, his tone sneering. "Way I heard it, they already tried it with some boys before me. Didn't take hold. City boys like me? Farmers? Didn't work then. Ain't gonna work for me. Ain't gonna work for you, neither, you a city boy 'n all."

He appeared to be speaking to John Henry in particular, the closest of his audience. My brother's eyes were as big as sunflowers.

As if to be certain John Henry was listening, Ralph added, "You from Brooklyn, right?"

John Henry nodded.

"What I thought. Now them country boys?"

Ralph continued. "Maybe. Maybe farmer works for them. It's what they know. But you?" He gazed at John Henry as if what he beheld was plain-as-day evident. "Uh-uh."

The toothpick traveled in his mouth as he collected his thoughts.

"You?" he said, John Henry leaning into his words. "Carpenter? Maybe. I could see that. Shoemaker? Why not? Could see that, too.

"But for me?" His voice rose, his thumb striking his chest. "Mechanics."

It was a word familiar to me, more by sound than meaning. I bumped a bit closer to better hear what Ralph had to say. Each "bump," I had to lift my hips to avoid snagging my white smock on a splinter. It was important to understand in case I had to counter any of his claims for John Henry's sake. If anyone knew I was there, they chose to ignore me.

"Mech – mechanics?" another little boy said, the sacrificial lamb for Ralph's scorn.

"Yeah, mechanics," Ralph said, as if speaking to a fool. "Fixing automobiles," accent on the *mo*. "Horses going, automobiles coming. Filling stations popping up everywhere. Well, not out here maybe. Not yet, anyway. But in the city? Take it from me, machines coming. What a man told me. That's where it's at, where it's going, don't you know? And I want a get there, see? Make me some real money."

"How you know all this?" John Henry said, his green-as-spring-grass voice rising. It was the same question clattering around in my head.

"How?" Ralph offered the knowing smile of

a church-wall saint. "Just look around. Well, not here, that's for sure. I mean in Brooklyn. Remember? Next time you make it home, take a look around. Everywhere you look, you'll see automobiles, right? What you see? More automobiles or less?"

"More," John Henry said to the set-up question.

"'At's right," Ralph said, flicking away the older worn toothpick and replacing it with his latest creation. "Give that boy a *cee*-gar. *More!* And motorized trucks for hauling. No more horses dropping you-know-what in the street."

A circle of giggles interrupted him, what he wanted, I believe.

"Gasoline engines. Steam engines," Ralph continued to hold forth, his eyes shining with the spirit of his belief. "Engines need a mechanic when they break down, which they always do. Man says to you, 'You a mechanic?' And I say, 'Heck, yes sir I am.' He says, 'How much it gonna cost me to fix my automobile?' And when I tell him, after his eyes pop out, and he blows up like a red balloon, he says, 'Okay, when can you fix it?' And you know why he says that? Because where he gonna go? To the mechanic, that's where."

Ralph knuckled himself in the chest once more while his audience rolled with laughter, one boy holding his belly.

To John Henry, Ralph said, "We got machines right here, Bub. Not engines, mind you, but machines. Harvesters. Separators out in the dairy. Things got wheels and axles, all the time breaking down. What I'm saying, you get the chance? Watch how they fix it. Learn. It's what I do.

"Better, find one ain't broke. Take it apart, put it back together, what I do, like I said. Do what you can here. Get it in that little bump you call a head so you'll be ready." He added a light pop to John Henry's forehead with his finger, and said, "Right here."

Again, the little boys rocked with laughter, no one harder than my brother. It all sounded so good.

"Got an old Ford engine back of the horse barn where they fix things," Ralph said. His lesson still running, he eased back into the telling. "Don't work none, but it's there, all rusted up. Study up on it like I do."

"Who lets you?"

I felt like a flushed rabbit who just heard a dog bark. The voice was mine. Fortunately, it did not disturb Ralph. If he even looked at me, I never noticed.

"Not who, Sis," he said, his eyes on John Henry. "It's how. You got to keep your eyes and ears open. And you got to ask, that's all. Let's say I find a man working on a busted axle, right? First thing I say to him, 'You mind if I watch, sir?' Don't forget the *sir*. And he might go like this."

Ralph shrugged, a big high-drama shrug.

"Or he might say, 'Long as you don't get in my way, I don't mind.' 'Cause he can see I'm interested in what he's doing. What you need to be," the finger again tapping my brother. "Interested.

"Minute or two goes by?" Ralph went on. "I can see he needs somebody to hold the axle tight while he works on one end. So I grab on, hold it steady. Next thing you know, he's saying, 'Hand me them calipers.'

"You know what calipers is, little man?" He spoke to John Henry, but it was for everyone as he was about to reveal his secret knowledge.

The revelation was only mildly disappointing.

"It looks like these little clippers you measure things with. Anyway, now I'm helping him, and he's explaining what he's doing to me. Teaching me. And why?"

"'Cause y'all interested," a boy from South Carolina said.

"That's right. 'Cause I'm *interested*," Ralph said. "Exactly! Give this boy a kewpie doll and a *cee-gar*, too. I can see I'm gonna run out a cee-gars."

Laughter again rumbled through his audience, mine included.

"Now," Ralph continued, tight to his task and loving it, "I'm helping this man, and he's helping me. You show interest in a man's work, he don't mind telling you about it. 'Pears to me, he's proud of it.

"And – and you can't be afraid to ask," Ralph insisted, his arm rising, finger pointed skyward. "Can't be afraid of 'No.' You won't hear it much, not after they see you're interested. You want to learn how to do something, ask. What I do. I ask, they most always show me."

"What about the old Ford?" a boy asked. It was not John Henry.

"Same thing," Ralph said, rising from the top step, brushing wood shavings from his pants. "I asked. Now? I go anytime I can. Tinker with it.

Squeeze a little oil in here, rub a little rust off there. Use every tool in the shop. Pull apart what I can, then put it back. I think I about got it figured out.

"Remember," he said, heading inside, "they want me able to care for my ownself. You too, Bub," he said to John Henry. Then pointing to others, "And you. And you. Well, *I* intend to, but not as no farmer. When they put me out the door, I want to be ready."

A while later, it was just John Henry and me, still talking on the porch. The others had followed Ralph inside. I could see the wheels turning in my brother's head. If not, he would have already been gone. I was just waiting, wanting to be sure he did not go off half-cocked. Maybe filled with thoughts he did not know what to make of. This was part of my promise to Mama.

"That Ralph, he's pretty smart," he said, at length. "You think he's smart, Bill?"

He could not say "Wilhelmina" when he was little. Called me "Willa," then "Bill." How he got there I do not know. But then, most adults could not say my name either. They'd say "Willamina" or "Willmina." It was too small to fuss over, trying to correct someone every time they messed up my name. Especially when they were adults and I was just a little kid.

I liked my name. It was part of who I am. Only people close to me called me "Bill." I would answer to it, but it was not me. I was "Wilhelmina."

"You think Ralph's smart?" John Henry repeated his question, bubble-popping me out of my thoughts.

"I think so," I said, "but I'm not certain. For

sure, it sounds like farming's not for him."

Good, hard work to grow up on, but maybe not to live on, I thought.

"You think I should be a mechanic?" John Henry said.

His seriousness demanded an answer from me that matched it. I thought, shoe repair? Carpentry? Brick laying? Maybe. "Mechanic" sounded good, but how much could John Henry learn about it at The Howard. They were not training boys in mechanics. It was too new. Was Ralph right about the future? About cars?

"Let me think about it some," I finally said to my brother.

That evening, after dinner, a meal lengthened by thinking on my part, I tried to answer his question.

"If they will teach it, okay. But what do you think?" I said. "Do you like taking things apart, putting them back together, getting grease on your hands?"

John Henry said, "I don't know."

"Okay. Well, what do you think you might want to do someday?" I was trying to help him to his own answer instead of telling him mine – which I did not have.

"Maybe be a fireman," he said, and disappeared into his own thoughts which I decided not to disturb. It was his turn to think.

Seems to me, I thought, that whatever you decide, if *you* decide it, it will be best.

Right at that moment, the issue of choice jumped up again, John Henry's many opportunities compared to mine. I brushed at it as I might a fly buzzing my face. I did not want to think about it at that moment. It brought me low if I plumbed it too deeply or too long. My task was to think about Ralph's words, and how they might affect my brother.

Was Ralph right? Engines? Machines? Not in Kings Park as far as I could see. In Brooklyn, yes, but we were not there.

John Henry would have to decide for himself. In the years to come, I would watch him, see what he tended toward. Maybe then I would know enough to answer his question.

Chapter Eight: Life at the Howard

Life at The Howard could be good. I do not want to sound as if I was sad a lot or cried myself to sleep. I was not, and I did not. (Well, maybe once or three times.) But mostly, I was happy with what was in front of me, what I was doing.

To be away from those you love and find a way to be happy, I had to think "short." Maybe the word I want is "small." Think too far back, sadness could overtake me, make it hard for me to move. Try to look too far ahead, I would become dizzy over what I could not see. Like staring too long at stars, wondering how they got there.

When you shorten everything? If there is a better way to put it, I need someone to please tell me. When you think "short," things are all right. Life becomes the things you do, sometimes no more than the thing you are doing. *That* short.

If I caught myself starting to think "long," you might call it "daydreaming," that was okay. Sometimes, I needed that, needed to work something through in my mind. But if sadness or dizziness began to creep in, I would start humming a song to block it. Most often, I would hum "Beautiful Dreamer."

On occasion, someone – a housemother, an inmate – would hear me sing-humming. If it was "Beautiful Dreamer," it seemed to put them in a better place. The housemothers probably grew up with the song. I would bet, when they heard it, it touched at something locked away in their hearts.

I remember a time when Mrs. Gordon, the Reverend's wife, heard me bird-chirping away. She smiled at me and said, "That's lovely, child."

Next thing I knew, she was humming it. And that made me smile. It seemed as if she did not know all the words. That or maybe she was keeping something private.

You might think that old song would take me back, maybe too far, into my past. It did not. It was the music, not the words. I scarcely knew them. No, it was the lilting, gliding, flowing music that carried me to a good place in the mind.

It was magical. The edges of my vision became violet. I would settle into whatever I was doing, humming more than singing. It never changed.

"Beautiful dreamer, wake unto me
Starlight and dewdrops are waiting for thee
Da da-da da da, da-da-da-da..."

That was about it with the words. It was even worse with the chorus.

"Beautiful dreamer, da-da da da..."

I once looked them up, the words, Mr. Stephen Foster's words. But I really did not try hard to remember them. I suspect I did not want anything to change the way I felt when I hummed the song. The music and the feelings were stitched together in a tight-seamed memory no sleeping powder could match.

At The Howard, it was hard to drift too far off. Things were organized with care, laid out like bridal clothes on a bed. You knew what came next, where you had to be and what you had to do.

For me, it was getting used to what was. I think I was good at that, staying in the right-now. Years later, I believe it helped me take to motherhood. Hard as it was sometimes, I loved it. Still do, more than ever.

The Howard in Kings Park was like being set down on an island, Indian Head Island, surrounded by an ocean of fields and woods. I would hear the wail of a train engine just beyond the horizon, pretend it was a boat horn. It was not hard to imagine Robinson Crusoe's trials. I too felt cut off from the world at times. Yet like Crusoe, what I found there was enough to live on, to survive. Now, I think, what drama! What an imagination!

An imagination can free you or trap you, depending. It can set you off from the world like an invisible wall, making it harder to live in. Or it can make it easier for you to live in a world you do not always understand. Thinking back, I believe it helped me, like having an old friend at hand.

The staff at "Indian Head Island" kept a close eye on us, especially with some of the girl-chasing older boys, their backdoor eyes and Saturday-night talk filling the air. My last year there (1915), they started noticing me a little. Or maybe it was more than a little and I did not know. That would have been okay with me because I was not ready for that.

Some of the things they would say, trying to be clever, were funny. Fortunately, more than believing any of it, I hardly knew what to make of it. Years later, even when I wanted to believe it, I somehow managed to keep my distance from fast talk.

"Little Princess" was one of the names they used when they were pestering me. John Henry and I tended to the short side. My whole family did.

I would hear things like, "Little Princess, where's your white gown? You going to the ball?"

I knew they were referring to the fancy dress I wore when The Quartette performed, but suspected it was more than that, more of what I did not want.

It might be "Little Princess" if they were interested, "Short Stuff" or "Shorty" if they were just passing time. I did not need to hear it, though. Their wolf-smiling eyes told the story.

Interested, I would hear, "When can I see you?" or "Maybe we could walk out sometime?"

First time I heard, "When can I see you?" I did not say anything. It was not my way to sass. But I thought, you can see me now. I am right here. It made me want to smile, but I did not. I did not want him to think my smile said, "I like your words."

If I had to be on an island, I am glad it was Kings Park. Glad it was Indian Head Farm. I felt safe there.

We would hear about a war going on in Europe, thousands of people dying, boats being torpedoed, poison gas. It would leave me uneasy, feeling the creep and crawl of fear. Reminded me of a wasp buzzing a screen door, searching for a way in. I would look around the farm, look at the slow-moving animals, calm in their own way, look at the fields running green to the dark-green hem of the woods, the blue sky, and I would calm, too.

In the safe place in my mind, sometimes the woods became "the forest." It would make me nervous, but not in a bad way. More like under-the-covers nervous when you read a fairy tale. Magical. Scary? Yes, but more the "scary" of a ghost story, not the horrid "scary" of poison gas and everyone dying.

It was not always easy to know where "safe" was for a child, especially for colored children. "Colored." What a funny, beautiful word! As a child, I did not think about it other than that was who *we* were. Now, I believe it was a safe word for white people when they had to think about us, a polite word when they had to talk about us.

"Safe" in the mind was knowing today could be like a good day yesterday, probably the same tomorrow. That was a comfort for colored people, one most of us did not have. Worrying about poison gas? There were places all over this country where colored people were dying from poisoned minds. Still are. It could come out of nothing, sudden-like, burn itself out and be gone – until the next time. We learned "next time" might be next minute. Good thing I had my safe place in the mind.

It was a white world outside Indian Head, but no one ever bothered us. Space and the fact that we stayed to ourselves probably protected us as much as anything. The only times we left The Howard were for very occasional outings. It might be a few of us or just one of the older inmates placed on a trial run. Most of those outings, I believe, were linked with fund-raising activities. Which was okay with me; we always needed more money to keep The Howard open.

But Kings Park was safe. No poison gas. The only other time I remember being scared something across the sea might hurt me arrived a few years later. 1918. Something called the Spanish Influenza came through like an invisible poison mist. Thousands died in America, millions across the world. *That* frightened me. They had stopped using poison gas, but nothing, it seemed, could stop this disease. It came, killed quickly and moved on. At times, I wondered if the whole world would perish.

Back in Brooklyn, we had to wait until the flu burned itself out. It might have been better to be at The Howard in Kings Park during that dark time. I could have looked out at Indian Head Farm and found peace.

It was too late by then. The Howard Orphanage and Industrial School was gone. It is funny – well, odd-funny, strange – when I was there, I always wanted to be home. Yet when I heard it had closed, I felt sad, like something living had died.

Chapter Nine: Anger? Yes. Hate? No!

I was always friendly. You might think otherwise from some of those old pictures, me staring as if I was looking through the camera. That was when I was little. They posed us that way at The Howard, real serious-like. Told us if we moved an eyelash, we would mess up the picture. Looking back, John Henry and I looked pretty grim. That was not our nature. But we were taught to obey adults. We were just being dutiful.

A couple of years later, my nature won out. I decided if I blurred the picture, so be it. From then on, you were going to see me smiling.

Someone once told us – a housemother, Mrs. Gordon? – it was easier to smile than frown. A smile needed fewer muscles. I did not know about the muscles, but I already knew a smile was the better way. It was just in me, who I was.

I was friendly with just about everyone, friends with a few. I probably held back a little. Maybe I thought I was keeping a drop of my love in reserve, saving it for my family.

The words "cautious" and "careful?" When you hear them, you might think they mean the same thing. But for me, there was a difference, at least the way I used them with people. I did not see myself as "cautious" at the beginning of friend-making. I was not hesitant to start. But once started, I tended to be "careful" until I could see what it was and how it was holding up. I did not rush headlong into it, doors and windows wide open. Rather, I eased into it, toe first in late spring water.

Maybe I wanted to be sure. I was open to people, but not bold with them. While I gave of myself to a possible friendship, I paid close attention to what came back.

Fortunately, I was friendly by nature, too. So much so, for me the difference between "friendly" and "friend," though narrow, is real. Best thing I can think of is a short bridge over a deep gorge. Narrow as it was, I guess what I am saying is the difference was still large.

There I go again, squeezing words, picking at them with tweezers until I get them right. But I mentioned earlier – will probably do it again – how important words are to me. Always were. I was taught to try to get them right, to utter them with care and a purpose. I was also taught that if I could not do that, not to say them.

So it was a strange time when I found myself struggling not to hate a girl named Frances. When she was around, anger was not far behind, trailing like, well, like poison gas. I tried *hard* not to let something bad taint my soul, but Frances was my test.

There was a darkness about Frances, far darker than her skin. A Southern girl, larger than me in all ways, she had her tightly curled hair, napped by nature, straightened. Painful as it must have been, she had it processed as often as they would allow.

I remember that because she always teased me about my "good" hair, as if I processed mine, too.

I stopped denying it, because it only seemed to wind her further into hatefulness. She never passed on a chance to comment about the color of my skin, either. Though she never said it outright, she would hint at my parentage, making it sound ugly.

One time, I told her, "You are right, my Mama's white."

That only seemed to make it worse, as if knowing rather than guessing fired her bitterness. So, no more comments from me after that.

Did it end when I said nothing? It did not. She would add a hateful stare to the teasing. Frances could out-stare anyone. It was not fun, but I could handle that better than getting caught up in "are too," "am not."

In 1915, flickers of womanhood beckoning to us, it got worse.

At first, I thought her resentment was that "green-eyed monster" I had heard about. That is what other girls who saw it thought. One of them said, "Oh, don't pay her no mind; she's just jealous."

When I tried to think of what she might envy, I could come up with nothing. My clothes? We both wore what was donated to The Howard. Family? We were both in an orphanage, were we not? My hair? My skin? Whatever it was, ill will seeped from her like oil from poison ivy.

In time, I came to wonder if it was something else, if something had happened to her. I just could not believe she had been made that way. Maybe someone she loved had let her down, and she could not bear the disappointment.

Her hate seemed to flare oven-hot after she

heard a boy call me "Princess."

"Princess!" She said it loud so anyone nearby could hear. It was so hateful, it was worse than scorn. "Princess? You? A princess? You a princess, then I'm the Queen of Siam."

What helped me in the end was finally understanding, it was not me causing the problem. Something lay crouched inside of her, something dark and unforgiving. It worked at her like a festering wound, infecting her soul. Scorching it. Whatever it was, it allowed her no peace.

I might have felt sorry for her had she not been so mean. It left me too angry to be merciful, and that was bad for me, too. It went against everything I had been taught, even my nature.

My test was not to let anger turn into hate. Anger towards me was something I was not used to. Sadly, with Frances around, it became familiar. But I was frightened of hate. I could see before me, in Frances, what it could do to a person, to her spirit. Hate ate at her like acid on anything. It is terrifying what it can do, how quickly it can destroy. I wanted no part of it.

I once overheard the housemothers chatting, swapping stories like playing cards. One of them was telling a story about a girl from Alabama by way of South Carolina. One of the inmates? At first, I was not sure. I was in the next room folding clothes. Could not help but hear. Did not try not to, either.

Two years earlier, the girl and her family pulled into a country town, packed onto a mule-drawn wagon. I do not know whether it was Alabama or South Carolina. A younger sister, no more than three, had a "fulminant" fever. I had no idea what the word meant at the time, but it sounded bad. It was.

They pulled up in front of a drug store hoping to get a cup of water for the sick girl, maybe find someone who might offer a medicine or direct them to a doctor. Sick as her sister was, the girl noticed her parents hold back for just a moment. While they were deciding who would go in and ask, she jumped down and entered the store. She found only a white boy in a white hat behind the fountain part of the store. There was no one at the drug counter.

She immediately explained her little sister's plight to the boy, and asked for a cup of water. The boy glanced around for a second, nervous-like, and filled a paper cup from the fountain. Just as he was handing it to her, the druggist appeared from behind a curtain. He was a little white man in a white coat. Plump, a fringe of reddish-brown hair "circled his head like a halo in a painting." He seemed not unkindly. (How could they know all that? It *must* have been one of the inmates.)

From behind thick glasses, he gazed at the scene. Then he took the cup from the boy's hand, and poured it in the sink, crushing the cup.

He said to the boy, "You know better 'n that."

To the girl, he said nothing, just looked at her for a moment and returned behind the curtain.

Later that day, under a "dusky-purple" sunset, her sister died. The girl was so angry, the loss seared that part of her that feels. She blurted to her grieving mother, "I *hate* that man."

"No!" her mother thundered, willing herself up through an ocean of tears, startling the girl. "Don't say that. Don't you ever say that. Don't even *think* that!"

After a moment, the mother dabbed at the stunned girl's eyes with a piece of cloth she had torn from her dress.

"If I let myself hate that man for what he did, I might have to kill him," her mother said. She spoke in a strange voice, one the girl barely recognized. "I can't let that happen and neither can you. Anger? Yes. Hate? *No!*"

I wondered if I had been standing in a draught during the story, chilled as I felt. The story drifted into other stories, but I lost track of them. I was still shivering from the mother's words.

Could it have been Frances they were talking about? That might help explain the iron ball of misery she toted everywhere. If it was Frances, she fell short of her mother's warning. But maybe try as she might, she just could not heed it. Maybe it was so bad, she tried to bury it deep inside. The hate may have been the oil seeping out, poison to the touch.

Hard as it was for my family, I had never known a hard time like Frances. Every family lost a child or knew someone who had. Children died all the time – but not because people did not try to save them. My life had been tested, but not shattered. My hopes lay in front of me, not crushed like a paper cup.

There were times – not many, I must admit – I tried to think of a way to reach out to Frances. But the burning wall of anger around her was too hot to get through. When I was upset about something, even angry, I wanted to get through it, not get even. The price Frances paid to swallow all that soul-charring anger, was, in the end, to hate. I was not about to pay that price.

Chapter Ten: Questions without Answers

Thoughts of losing a child set off an explosion of memories, feelings and questions. So many questions. Some of them left me distressed, unsure what to do with them, especially the questions.

I was not one to run and bleat them to someone else. Rather, I tried to work them out for myself, if I could. When I could not, I would try to put them up on a shelf in my mind. Leave them for now, let them mellow a bit, look at them later. There are some things in this world you have to stop thinking about, at least for a while. If you do not, they can leave you frozen, unable to move. I am speaking of the questions that seem to have no answers.

Church was a central point in my life, but more so after my marriage to John F. Hamlin. How could it not be? My father-in-law, Reverend John W. Hamlin, was the pastor of Mount Lebanon Baptist Church. He and his wife, Frances, brought me into a family that lived a Godly life. I would like to say "welcomed me" but that would not quite do. It was through their church that I met my future husband.

It seemed a natural continuing of the life I had lived until then. All those years at The Howard, Sunday services were a fixture, as were daily religious devotions. From the outset, its foundation lay upon Christian charity and concern for colored children. At the heart of this ideal was religious education. The superintendent was Reverend James H. Gordon and his wife the "matron." Further, the Board of Trustees and Managers always contained a sizable number of ministers.

Chapel services were held daily together with religious instruction and rules for inmates' worship behavior. Sleeping was forbidden. Should you forget or just drift off, you could expect to be awakened, and not gently. Still, there was no way to prevent thinking or daydreaming. I did my share of both. In those surroundings, filled with moral lessons, thoughts of life and death were common. At least, they were with me. I would expect that could be true for most people. If not, you must have mastered the art of sleeping with your eyes wide open.

If there was one rule above all others, it was that you did not question. You accepted His will. In my heart, I did accept it, but often, like an uninvited guest, a question would tip-toe in. You may not want him there, but there he is. A wayward uncle, perhaps, who lives out of a woven suitcase, washes his shirt at night so he can wear it the next day, sucks on a hard candy to hide the tang of whiskey. You would try to be kind, but no matter what, you would have to grant he is there.

Child loss was one of those questions that set off a never-ending war within me. I could not answer it, could not find my way to an armistice. I would hear explanations in church and out that just did not satisfy. The worst was "God's will." God's will? Would the loving God I believe in *will* the stillborn birth or early death of His own creation? I had no answer, but "God's will" was not it for me. It left me troubled, surrounded as I was with so much child death.

"It has always been thus," a minister once declared, preaching his sermon. "It is not ours to question, but to accept." Or something like that.

Why? my brain whispered.

At The Howard, I sometimes wondered if someone might hear my thoughts, strong as they were. *Accept*? It sounded as if what happened was okay. It was not okay. I thought there needed to be a different word, one that was fair to the lost child. Back then, I was not up to the task. That I was even thinking those questions, questioning His will, left me uneasy.

A few years later, I decided that "to live with it" was the best I could do. I did not "accept" it, never would. Maybe "accept" made it easier for some to quiet a bad memory or even forget it. I did not want to forget it. But I could learn to "live with it" like you do all painful memories. They have their place along with the good. That would have to be my acceptance. If not, so be it.

Sometimes, the question just appeared, quiet as a snail. One minute it was not there, the next – where did that come from?

My last year at The Howard (1915), I began thinking about having my own children someday. Questions began to collect about the scary thought of losing one. Most of the inmates had lost brothers or sisters. Although she seldom talked about it, most of my mother's children from her first marriage died in childhood. I could not bear to imagine what that must have done to her.

As a child, the questions left me nervous even when they were not scaring me. I was taught not to question God's will. But I did. Again, the questions were just there. Even if I did not want them to be, they were. Years later, I came to believe I was not challenging His will. He gave me a mind to try to answer questions – and to question.

When I was first married, I would, on occasion, bring a question or a concern to my in-laws. My father-in-law, Reverend Hamlin, whose faith seemed unquestionable, encouraged me never to be afraid of questions. I sensed from him that faith was what anchored us to belief when we dared explore questions. At the same time, he seemed so set in his beliefs, there was little room for disagreement. In time, I stopped bringing my questions to him.

To his credit, he would not simply tell me *the* answer, even though I believed *he* believed he knew it. Rather, he would place the task of understanding His purpose back on my shoulders. He would not tell me how to think. It was up to me as to how I would use God's gift, to answer my questions if I could or find a way to live with them if I could not. Amazing in someone so strong in his beliefs, and dare I say, opinions.

I never was able to answer questions surrounding child loss or the suffering of families when a child passed. In time, I was able to live with them uncomfortably, never easily, never denying them, but live with them.

It might sound like my faith was fickle, up or down, depending upon the day and what was going on. Not so. No matter how I might think about it, my faith abided. To question God is to believe in Him, not to deny Him. A pillar of my faith was my belief that someday I would be able to answer those unanswerable questions.

Somewhere, another sermon likely, maybe I read it, it was said that while "seeing is believing, faith is believing absent evidence."

I pray. If you pray, you must have faith. Otherwise, to whom do you pray? But sometimes, I pray too much when I want something to happen and not enough at others. That brings to mind the word "hypocrite." Heard it in many sermons. I do not like to think of myself that way. What to do? Do I pray even more for something? Pray for Him to remove that bad thought? Or do I make up my mind to do something about it myself? From my words, I think you can tell which way I tilt.

I read somewhere Mohammedans pray five times a day, no matter what. Faith. They figure out in which direction Mecca lies, roll out their prayer mats, and bow to Him. I am certain I do not want to pray that much. But I would feel better if I did it every day, not just when I want something.

Well, I *do* pray every day. Maybe what I am trying to say is, I could offer gratitude more on in-between days. Days where I am not asking for something, but just saying "Thank You" for this life. Anyway, faith.

But I was still a thinker. I would like to believe when I do that, think, I am celebrating a God-given gift.

After The Howard, as I found my way into

adulthood, I continued to make use of the gift. Freer to have my thoughts, I would set up debates in my mind. I would test myself, posing questions without hesitation (well, maybe a little), weighing answers without fear (again, maybe a little). More than ever, I understood the right to think your own thoughts can never be taken from you.

When my children began to arrive, my time for journeying by thought came less often. Wondering became like recess in school, filling the narrow, and narrowing, spaces between responsibilities. Like prayer, I find a way to it every day.

Fortunately, I was blessed with a good husband. With a growing family, Sundays were a time of great effort before church. Children had to be bathed and dressed properly. John helped at a time when not all men did. Once at church, during the service, they had to be tended while adults worshipped. That is where the church community stepped forward. Reaching out to distract a busy child here, hold a sleeping child there, we still managed to sing, testify, and pray.

And pray I did.

Chapter Eleven: Weeksville

It might come as a surprise to know that I lived in a very sheltered world. One might wonder, a colored girl growing up in 1910, a young woman in the 1920's? But for the most part, my world was protected. And yes, it was almost absent white people. The cure for injury from outside was the family, the church, the community, the bosom of our lives.

At The Howard, we were more sealed off from whatever the outside world might present. Even the little town of Kings Park, just a short trip up Indian Head Road, was a world away. Our play-house universe was the campus, the farm, and the surrounding woods, a colored world by and large. It extended into, but not beyond the woods. With rare exceptions – a delivery here, an event there – the few whites that visited were board members. Dressed formally for the most part, they were educated, dignified, and supportive, if apart.

When they arrived to review us, we were dressed in what finery we had, directed to "behave." It was that and more if potential donors visited. If we had owned a red carpet, we would have rolled it out for them and strewn it with rose petals. We would have worn lavender sachets on our wrists and sprayed the air lilac. We would have done almost anything to convince them of our worth. Well, of *their* worth in supporting us.

Otherwise, The Howard was our world. The only time the outside world might intrude was when a placement did not work out. One of the older inmates – usually but not always a boy – might return trailing a tale of unhappiness. Placed with a white farmer, he would tell us about a life of over-work and under-appreciation.

In one instance, an older boy (another William) told us, "Felt like I was back in Virginia. Man treated me like a field-hand. Felt more like a slave than a wages man."

It never touched me. I was twelve in 1915 when I returned to Brooklyn. For me, all those years, the orphanage was a safe world.

But in Brooklyn, Weeksville was the mother love, the bower of safety we all need. I was never happier than when I was there. I was home.

Chancing beyond the limits was a risk to my sense of order, to the church's teachings, to myself. There were no lines or signs "Beware, Danger Ahead," but I knew.

I heard somewhere, maybe I read it, that Weeksville was a colored community from the beginning. True or not, it was a favored place for colored people, a good place to grow up. Hard? Yes, sometimes, but a good place.

I believe everyone needs a good place to grow in, a place where self-respect can blossom. For colored people, for *me*, it was a place not reckoned by white judgment and eyes with legs.

The embrace of this world only increased after my marriage in 1920 to John F. Hamlin. My husband was the oldest son of the seven surviving children to Reverend John W. and Frances Walker Hamlin. My in-laws were Godly people, upstanding in all that word might suppose. Their beliefs were unbendable as Pittsburgh steel, but their loving concern sun-shined forth from Mt. Lebanon Baptist Church. For the church community, it was no different at the parsonage on Sackman Street.

My husband and his siblings, all raised within the church, were also good people. They were not perfect. Who amongst us is? But they were good, loving people, the way we can be. The way we can be at our best, the way we were meant to be, caring about each other.

I came to believe our community returned my father-in-law's preachments, his dignified spirit, his love. Have you ever been around someone like that? It can make you nervous about making a mistake and displeasing him. But it can also make you take measures of yourself to try to be better.

Weeksville was not paradise. It had its dark moments, as in any community on Earth: drunkenness, gambling, arguing, even violence. But they were like a distant backfire from a Ford automobile compared to the steady throb of love. No more than a bubble "Pop!" in the stream of life. Weeksville was my heart's rest as well as my home.

While life was fairly basic and never easy in Weeksville, it was good. What you needed was there for the most part, a place to live, heat in winter, ice in summer. Neighborhood markets supplied clothing, sundries, food. Carts slipped in everywhere they could squeeze, selling fruits, vegetables, even flowers. If the market did not have it, you could find it on a pushcart, and fresher. Had a taste for ripe strawberries in the spring? You just found the right cart and bought a quart.

In the heart of Weeksville, St. Mary's Catholic Hospital provided medical help. They did not discriminate, at least not by policy. It always came down to people, sometimes to a person.

We heated our home and I cooked with coal. It was delivered down a chute into our basement. John would shovel it into the furnace before the superintendent, "the super," woke up. That or carry up a bucket for me to cook with. Only the super was supposed to fuel the furnace. Once he discovered he could sleep late and wake up to a warm apartment, he told John, "Go ahead." If John was away at work, I did the shoveling or toting, no problem.

Ice? Sometimes they delivered, sometimes you had to get it yourself at the icehouse. It depended on how busy they were or how badly you wanted it. Some people had rolling dollies or little wagons to carry their ice. We would just tie a rope around the ice-block, wrapped in burlap, and drag it home. In winter, whatever you wanted cold – jello, pudding – you put it outside on a window sill until it chilled.

It was a busy time, especially after our children started arriving. You still had your work to do with childcare on top of it. My secret? Try to make two one. (My math again, maybe a little magic, too.) When they were babies, I would talk to them or sing while I bathed them. Same thing when I did the wash or a dozen other things I had to do.

Now that they are old enough, I turn the

words or songs into games. "Ring around the Rosy" is a favorite. When they all fall down at the end, they laugh so hard, they chicken cackle. "London Bridge is Falling Down" is another one they love. Among the sing-songs, "Itisket-Itasket" and "Mary Had a Little Lamb" are most loved. For them it *is* magic; for me, sheer joy.

At times, the little girl in me jumps out so much, I can barely concentrate on my work. Is it worth it? And how!

Weeksville was not *our* world, it was *the* world. Churches, schools, businesses? You walked to them. If it was too far to walk, you found a trolley. Our lives did not change much. Families, friends, church members? We lived in the same neighborhood, there or nearby. A map might say we belonged to "Crown Heights" or that "Bedford-Stuyvesant" had a claim on us. But it did not matter what a map said or did not say, for me, it was *Weeksville*.

It might have been different had we had to go out in the wider world. Not might have, *would* have. Work, the need for it, drew some of us outside our community. Those who did go beyond those invisible lines risked facing all that was wrong in the world. Each time, they had to square up to living at the mercy of its dangers.

For all I thought, I did not think much about the world outside Weeksville, not until I was grown. During the years in Kings Park, when my thoughts traveled beyond The Howard, they winged right back to Weeksville. To *home*.

On occasion, I might hear people talking, in

church or out. Might hear certain words swollen with meaning for colored people. *Equality. Racialism. Segregation. The NAACP.* Okay, the last is not a word, but for me it is. As a little girl, those words could flit like yellow butterflies. Catching my attention, they flew off before I could bring them into focus like a camera, maybe study them.

Once a young woman, the words advanced more like green caterpillars. They lingered in my sight-line, moving, stopping only after an incident – someone denied a house or a job. All movement ceased, all breathing, even time, when I would hear or read about a Southern lynching. So horrible, I will let it speak for itself, since time and words cannot.

I sometimes wondered how far away "The South" was. Hundreds of miles or just a few blocks?

We lived in this lively neighborhood, bustling with life, people just going about the business of living. For the most part, it was a happy community. Come to church on Sunday, you would know. Yet, just a few blocks in the wrong direction – *any* direction – your life could turn upside down. The shock when you understood this reminded you, deep down, of something you always knew, could never risk not knowing. It was like spotting a snake. No one had to say anything. You saw it, and stepped carefully.

I guess this is what fear does. In one lesson, it teaches you forever.

When we had to travel outside Weeksville, it was as if we were preparing for a funeral. We might have been going to a museum or to shop, but you would never have known. Bodies were scrubbed red, shoes shined to mirrors, bowlers brushed. Clothes were lint-picked and pressed into creases that could cut, hair-parts razored straight.

Preparation of the mind was even more thorough. Adults became quieter, even solemn, more edgy with children. I know I did – and do. We were preparing *not* to see suspicious eyes, *not* to hear rudeness or worse. I believe we feared discourtesy more than physical injury. It could come from anywhere or nowhere, a policeman or a shop owner.

The question might arrive in standard form. "Can I help you?" But the message was in the eyes, the pinched faces, as well as the dry voices. "What are *you* doing here?"

Tensions rose as we neared our destination. We tended toward pained, somber silence or false jokiness, laughing too hard at anything. I tended toward the silent side, pretended I wore horse blinders, could see only what lay in my path. Nothing really helped. You took in the sights or got your business done, and headed home. First thing upon arriving home, you exhaled, as if you had been holding your breath the whole time.

More than anything, I believe people want respect. The withholding of it may be the deepest hurt.

Those words the NAACP puts out, the causes it stands for or against? I have thought about them, but not in an all yes-or-no way. *Integration* for instance. Some of us want it, others do not. Me? I am not so sure. When I try to think about it, I feel spraddled over a fence, and cannot get off.

But *equality*? Yes! *Opportunity*? Yes, and

yes again! Otherwise, I want to be left alone, allowed to live my life in peace. I want the same for my children.

Now that women can vote, I find myself on that fence again. I read pamphlets from the NAACP urging colored people to register and vote, women as well as men. Sometimes, I hear it in church, too, my father-in-law's sermons no exception. He wants us in it, all the way. I do not know why, but it makes me excited and wary at the same time. I know it is a right thing to do. But it also pushes at me to move outside that safe world in my mind.

I will admit, I have been putting it off. Politics are so new to me. There is much I do not know. But I believe come next year, I will try it out locally, get my feet wet as they say. My big goal is for the 1932 Presidential Election.

I mentioned to my husband that I did not think a great deal of Mr. Hoover. "It just appears to me he has not done much to help people in need."

"Man couldn't do any less than the two came before him, Coolidge and Harding. One was always going on vacation, and the other? Every day in the White House *was* a vacation." He laughed when he said it, but there was no humor in his voice or his face.

It seems to me Mr. Hoover understands only the community he lives in. And here I am talking about the community I live in. But as President, is it not up to him to understand as many communities he serves as possible? In my mind, that would include Weeksville. *If* I vote, that is one thing I will be thinking about.

Chapter Twelve: Rules

Rules. They are always there. Even if you do not know them, you sense them. You follow them. Most often, they are of your own making.

I make beds every day. I brush my teeth. I iron out wrinkles from our clothes. Those and about a thousand others are my rules. Someone might say, "Those are not rules, they are just mindless habits we follow. *You* follow."

I would say, "You are right." But they are *my* rules. No one forces them on me. No one insists I follow them, not now as a woman. I choose to do them because they feel right.

Yet, for every rule I follow, I bet there are two or three I am not even aware of. In church, I sit or stand, depending. I do it automatically, without conscious thought. Habits? Maybe. But as a child, they were taught to me as rules. And as a child, they went unquestioned. We followed them as adults insisted, trusting they were showing us the way.

Then there are the rule breakers. The ones who lift the left foot instead of the right, peek too early, sing off key. Thinking back to The Howard, most of the time it was funny. They would trade a peck of trouble for a barrel of laughs. But now, looking back, it seems to me they were following rules, too – their own. If you always turn left when you are supposed to turn right, you are following a command. And what does that come from? A rule.

So in some ways, the rule breakers were following rules as much as the rest of us.

I pretty much always followed the rules. It was just in me to do so. My nature was not rebellious. I was a truster, though my eyes were open. Separation from my parents left me watchful.

At The Howard, most of us followed the rules. It was not a problem for me. They helped me fill the hole (never completely) away from my parents. I knew what to expect, where I was supposed to be, and what I was supposed to do.

On occasion, I did wonder about some of them – visitation for certain. But I did not begin to question them until much later. When the questions first arose, I believe I just noticed them and tucked them away. At some point, the questions lingered, and I began to think about them, after I had left The Howard.

Now, as a woman, I have both the safety and the freedom to ask, "Why do we do it this way?" Or "Is that the best way to do it?" I might have had the freedom back then to ask the question – if I could have gotten it into words. But it – *I* – did not feel safe brooking an adult. At least, that is how they might have received it had I taken it upon myself to ask. And I was not a rule breaker.

At The Howard, it seemed to me there were two types of rule breakers. I am not speaking of the occasional accident, but of those who deliberately broke rules. One type seemed normal to me, what I sensed more as a spirited moment than a willful trespass. The other was more an act of pure disobedience, willfulness the intention.

Margaret, a playful fifteen, had the spirit of something slightly wild. She made me think of a mustang. I have read about wild horses in the West. Except she was not really wild like that.

She was not pretty the way boys like, but there was a beauty about her that danced in with her spirit. "Pretty" you see, "beauty" you feel. To me, "pretty" is for right now, "beauty" forever. Margaret was beautiful, the bees knees and then some.

She loved to laugh, and get others laughing. Never in a mean way, she could mimic any adult at The Howard, including the directors whenever they came. She was especially good at "white" speech. More than words, it was the way she toned the sound as it came out, that and the way she would posture. She would capture someone with a lifted eyebrow, a poked-out stomach or crinkled lips. When she added the voice, there was no need to guess who. She slayed us, sending us into hysterics each time.

The housemothers, trying to bridle her like one of those mustangs, would get after her. I once heard one of them say they "needed to break a spirit sometimes to save a person." It sounded to me like they were talking about horses.

To Margaret they would say things like, "Keep this up, no man is going to want you someday." She might mumble, "That's okay. I don't want no man," setting us off again. But she did not do it out loud like backtalk. She had fire in her, but it was a life-loving glow, not a burn-the-house-down evil.

Now Sam? He was a horse of a different color. His name was Samuel, but you risked a knuckle punch in the arm if you called him that. So, "Sam" it was. Unlike Margaret, who was playful, Sam was a rebel, always in trouble. While I would not say he was evil, you never knew what he might do next – only that he would do something.

Sam could not sit still. He always had to be doing something. Unfortunately, that something was other than what the rest of us were supposed to be doing. Reverend Gordon, the matron, and the housemothers regarded him as willful, his disobedience deliberate. I am not so sure. True, he was disrespectful (mostly hidden), but to me, he was just different. They saw him as trouble, but I felt he was as much troubled. His rebellious behavior seemed almost beyond his control. In fact, I am not certain it was rebellion so much as he could not help it, at least some of it.

Almost seventeen in 1915, Sam was closing in on the end of his time at The Howard. We all knew they were having trouble placing him. He might just up and walk off a job or sass someone if he was of a mood. Sam would do just enough bad that it shaded the rest of what he was. He was even funny at times. But unlike Margaret, who stirred things up to create joy, Sam just did whatever he was going to do. It did not matter if it upset people (which it usually did).

They taught the girls to sit with our knees together, to be "lady like." Margaret would let hers slip slightly apart until she got someone giggling. Sam, on the other hand, might slip a bug down someone's collar. Or he might trip someone, pretending they just fell down. He sometimes ran off and hid in the woods, setting off great concern at The

Howard. He would then walk in, acting as if he had no idea why everyone was so disturbed.

Both of them, Margaret and Sam, seemed to crave attention. But I believe Margaret's rule-testing gifted others with laughter. Sam's antics seemed aimed at allowing him – and only him – to laugh

A rumor passed through the cottages like January wind off Long Island Sound. In desperation, the staff had confronted Sam with the picture of a murdered colored man down South. They asked him, "Is this how you want to end up?"

They tried to shock him, hoping he would straighten out. It did not work. When asked why he behaved the way he did, he just shrugged. When they tried to talk to him, he refused to grant them his eyes. They said he was "bad." I did not see him as all bad – some yes, but again, mostly just different. I know they feared for him in a way they did not for Margaret, that he would end up in trouble outside The Howard.

I felt sad when they sent him back to Brooklyn. I do not think Sam understood there are always rules wherever you go. You can laugh at them, try to ignore them, even run from them, but they are still there. I hope he found a way to live with them.

The rules I struggled with most at The Howard involved visitation. To the inmates, visitors were a scrap of bread to a starving puppy.

I did not fully understand it then, but looking back the rules seemed set up to discourage visitation.

There was a list for all to see: "Rules & Regulations for Visitors to Inmates." I only remember a few, but I can still see them like letters cut in a bronze door plate. *Regular visitations are the first Thursday each month, 1:30-4:30 PM.* How about, *Visitors not allowed on Sunday?*

Thursday, yes; Sunday, no. Thursday? What about working people? And Sunday? In a 5½ or 6 day work week, Sunday was the only day working people might have off. Some of the inmates had few enough visitors as it was. Those rules only made it harder. I would even say, almost impossible.

I only knew that John Henry and I so badly wanted to see our parents. As hard as it was for us, it must have been very hard for them. I suspect they tried to live with it because The Howard offered something they could not give, an education and training. For colored children, that was something where often there was nothing.

Over the years, I have tried to bring it up with my mother. I would brush lightly against it in conversation, testing the water. But she seemed so uncomfortable with it, with the past, I would say no more. It was not hard for me understanding how much her past was filled with grief. She had lost two husbands and most of her children, including John Henry. I will try to talk about that later.

At twelve, I knew I was not like Sam. I wished I could have been a little bit more like Margaret, but it was easier watching her.

I realize now, the staff was afraid for Sam and Margaret, of what might happen to them outside. More than they could say, I believe they were afraid for all of us outside The Howard. Whenever we went on an outing, to swim at The Sound or sing at an event, the rules increased.

I understand now, they wanted to protect us. But in a way, we were always on a stage, performing. "See the little colored children. Nothing to be afraid of." But when I think of Margaret, I still wonder how you can fear laughter. I would be more afraid if there were none.

Chapter Thirteen: The Daydream

To live a sheltered life as I did had to do only with what went on around me. Living among colored people, I was rarely touched by the frightening madness of racial hatred. But that spread-open umbrella could not protect me from my own thoughts and imaginings.

As a young child, bad dreams would swoop in on me like bats in the night. Age six, seven, eight – those were probably the worst years for terrifying dreams. Haunts seemed to jump up without reason. Someone chasing me, I cannot run fast enough. I am about to run down into a black unknown. Locked in a building, I cannot find my way out. They were all there. At The Howard, I might have had to cry it out against a housemother's skirted knee. But they passed with time, the terrors melting away like water in sun as those dreams seem to do.

At this point in my life, I sleep soundly. With five children, and our sixth on the way, there is no energy to spare for a nightmare. (I will try to speak later about why one of the five is living away from us now.)

One dream, a daydream, never passed. It remains with me to this day, can come upon me whenever I allow it. Or summon it. It started my last year or two at The Howard, probably let loose by pictures in a book, pictures of slaves.

In 1915, we were only fifty years beyond

slavery. In September 1929 as I write about my life, there are still living human beings who began their lives as slaves.

My daydream is of an old man, African, skin moonless-night black, at least in his seventies. He is sitting on a cabin threshold. Had I seen him in a picture? Maybe a photograph? I cannot remember, but I could not find the picture when I looked for it in books. His right shoulder is against a jamb. The timbers of the doorway are axe-cut, splintery, hard, but he is unmindful of the roughness. Leaning on one hand, the other is draped over a bent knee, gripping an unlit, corncob pipe. Was he about to light it? Was the photograph a trespass into what little privacy he owned – if he owned anything?

His hair and beard are short but scruffy. Unless someone helps him, he probably barbers them by feel. My mind says he is alone and does it himself. If there was a wife, he outlived her. That or she was sold away from him. The hair and beard are not cottony white but more the ash of cremated bone.

He is shoeless, his knobbed feet callused harder than a walnut. The bottom of one of them faces the camera. Was he too tired to turn it away? Or was this an act of defiance in the face of something uninvited and unwanted?

His wrinkled, white, collarless shirt – linen, linen and wool? – is open at the throat. The cotton he once picked too good for him to wear. The shirt is tucked into worn, calf-length trousers, shrunk almost to breeches from too many washings. He is probably not the first to own them, but likely the first man to repair them. The trousers are secured at his narrow waist by a length of rope. His shirt sleeves are rolled up, revealing bony forearms, veined like train-yard tracks.

Everything about him physically is spare. He is so thin, a scar on the arm holding his pipe seems like something worn, a bangle perhaps. But in its jaggedness, it is clearly not an adornment.

Most notably, his eyes, glistening mineral dark, stare at the camera. He knows his picture is being taken. It matters not to him, he is not posing. He will not. Life has taken almost everything he has to give, giving little in return. He refuses to give more. So determined is he, if a fly landed on his face, he might not move.

The eyes at first seem empty, as if the tenant moved out, but they are not. Centuries of knowledge, of *knowing*, mill behind them like a camped army. I find myself wanting to move to the side of the picture, away from the weight of those eyes. The accusation in them could set fire to a conscience – if it could find one.

If there is a message in that frozen stare, he will not reveal it. His life has been lived, endured, entirely as a slave. There is no one else in the picture. He appears alone.

Why the dream appears or I call it to me, I am uncertain. Want may have played its part in the lives of my parents, but slavery or bondage did not. My father's family traced free, Northern roots back well before the Civil War. There was no memory of slavery, but it had to have started where history vanished in the past. My mother's family came from Ireland by way of England, likely seeking opportunity. At an earlier time, they might have arrived bonded to someone, but in their case, they were free.

Yet the picture remains, the daydream still comes, summoned or not. Whenever I let myself think about it for more than a moment, I begin to breathe heavily. I begin to imagine his life. I refuse to shake it away, my head begins to swirl and swoon, and I have to sit. Even then, I hesitate to drift too deeply into his world. When I do, I circle toward feelings that leave me shaken, feeling faint, so tired I can barely move. Too tired to pull myself out of it, I continue to sink, a feeling of dread growing within me. Sometimes, I feel like I am under water, struggling for the surface, fearful I might not make it.

I promise myself, I will not do that again. But comes the dream, that moment of day drift, and I feel that spellbinding pull. At some point, I will likely surrender to it once more, as if moving toward a duty.

What am I imagining that is so frightening? A day in his life. Any day. From first light to sundown, a day with no more than tiny hopes, none that involves freedom.

I imagine him in his fifties, up *before* muster, a point of pride. He will start his day on his terms, a small victory among so many empty spaces. A breakfast of pan-fried bread or corn grits and molasses to keep him. He moves gingerly into intense Southern heat, testing it as one might water before entering it.

He will work for six hours before a noontime break. No longer a field hand, he never forgets years of labor – standing, bent and kneeling. It left him stooped, his limbs gnarled as tree roots. The elements completed what the work left unfinished.

He now toils driving a cart through the tobacco fields, carrying cut leaves to the curing barns. While the cart fills, he remains exposed to the merciless sun, a broad-brimmed hat his only shade.

Midday, he will rest for several hours until the sun is past its killing peak. Not seldom during his *rest*, he is "asked" to help at one of the drying sheds. He will bind leaves to be lifted to the rafters. Sometime after three, he will return to his field route and work until last light. Before returning to the cabin to tend to himself, he is expected to put up the mule, feeding, watering and currying the animal.

At his cabin, he has barely enough energy to put together a meager dinner. When he can, he will perk up his evening meal with fish he catches on Sunday. He will salt a fish to preserve it through the week, if he has enough from his allotment.

At twilight, I sense there is a wife there, though I never see her, not even a shadow. In the picture, there is not even a lingering sentiment to suggest she is still with him.

What I do see, in that absence of energy, is a nightly duty. From a bucket of unheated water, he damps the back of his weather-creased neck with a wet rag. Sitting with his eyes closed, he then washes his hands and feet. This occurs at the end of each day before he eats his meal – if he has the energy to eat. Whether he eats or not, he performs the ritual. Perhaps it is another tiny victory.

I chill at the thought that he retires to his

pallet of straw knowing tomorrow will be like today.

I wonder, in what did hope lie? Was there a *where*? Was freedom still something he could imagine? How did a feeling become form in his mind? If so, at what point did it pass? In those tunneled-from-rock eyes that have witnessed too much, that appears to be the case. All that remains is raw knowledge and cold fury.

He appears to have been deemed too old to work. Was that the case? Or was he judged capable of one more task equal to his brittle physical capacity, trying to squeeze one last drop of water from a dry cloth? It brought to mind an old Eskimo woman chewing hides to soften them. Once her teeth failed, now valueless, she was set out on an ice floe, released to the ages. Was the cabin his ice floe?

If he had been judged too old for labor, what had he been "freed" to do? Sit? Think about his life? The holes in it? The parts that went missing? The parts that never happened? Free to look out on the same scene as yesterday, and the day before, and the day before that, the only changes the elements by season?

Had he been allowed to garden behind the cabin? "Granted" a tiny patch where he might add tomatoes, okra, corn, onions, collards, beans, herbs to his meager diet? If so, did the colors stir his senses, maybe lift his spirits? Did they hearten him to plant flowers just for the delight of color – orange marigolds and day lilies, yellow daffodils, blood-red salvia? Maybe welcome blue morning glory to a slapdash trellis? Or would the glory of color have roused blunted hope too painful to bear in a creaking, settling body?

Was he allowed to fish? To berry – gathering blue, black or strawberries as seasons offered? And if so, was he *able* to?

This is what happens when I travel to him in my mind. Thoughts fly out faster and faster, more quickly than I can sort them. It is like opening a storage closet, and having the contents spill out all over you. How do you order them so you can put them back? I cannot. It is like trying to count stars. I finally have to shut my eyes.

To slow my flooding thoughts, I try to concentrate on one thing. I might focus on his pipe. The next thing I know, here I go again. Did he smoke or was it merely something to hold on to, something real to grip? If so, was he allowed tobacco for his pipe? Or did he have to fill it with a less satisfying substitute amid a wealth of tobacco?

Were there any joys – marriage, fatherhood, celebration of his skills? Did he have moments where he might, ever so briefly, permit himself a tiny sliver of pleasure? And could he allow himself the luxury of feeling it, knowing it could be erased on a whim? Could he risk allowing himself to love, knowing that could be simply severed like a limb? What could he possess?

If he could speak, what would he say?

See what I mean. I can only bear to think about it in tightly controlled bits. Any longer, my mind would start to seize. A frightening gloom would follow, falling over me like a mourning dress, my mood plunging. And yet, if only in those spurts, I felt the need to think about him. In honoring his life,

I was paying respect to a life that fifty years ago could have been mine.

Too far into those thoughts left me lightheaded, feeling faint, afraid to go on. Caught in the whirlpool, I was also afraid to stop, guilt threatening me if I did. Yet I could not yield to them, not with children to care for, their spirits in need of tending. I could not risk my own spirits by circling in too far, and losing my way out.

Nor could I speak of my daydream to anyone, not my beloved husband, not my father-in-law, no one. I feared what might happen if, in circling in, I opened Pandora's Box. Feared what it might do to someone else. I chose to be responsible for my thoughts, tending them as one might a forgotten gravesite.

Chapter Fourteen: My Lot

As a child, I noticed differences in the lives of boys and girls, but I did not think much about them. Around twelve, my last year at The Howard, that began to change. It was more than our activities, what we were allowed to do (boys played baseball, girls did not). I began to think about a person's lot in life. With age, those thoughts gained wings and wind.

Neither a man's nor a woman's lot is easy. I have heard women say, "A man's lot is easy." I know it was said in comparison to a woman's. To that, I say, "Applesauce."

I mean you can always compare them. You can compare anything with something else. But I believe that when you do, you can lose sight of your own truth.

And yes, if I compare them, a woman's lot might seem harder by its want of choice. Unless women were educated beyond elementary school, their choice was to marry or work as a domestic. Another example of my math: When you add one housewife and one domestic, what do you get? One domestic. Once more, $1 + 1 = 1$. Nifty, eh? Okay, I am laughing – sort of.

In the 1920's, it is slowly changing. Women with high school diplomas can become telephone operators or saleswomen in department stores. With college, they can teach or enter nursing. (Of course, for little or no pay, we taught and nursed in the past, but requirements are rising.) Now that we have the vote, maybe we can change it more.

But in 1929, a woman with an eighth grade education can marry, enter domestic service or char at night. (Why nighttime? That is when office buildings are cleaned.) Let me see – marriage, domestic work or charwoman? $1 + 1 + 1 = 1$. If she is lucky, she might find garment-factory work sewing. $1 + 1 + 1 + 1 = 1$. And this is a woman who likely can read, write and cipher, like yours truly. It might sound a tad bitter, but I can feel the corner of my mouth curling into a smile.

My point is that, yes, a woman's lot is not easy, but neither is a man's. Regardless of choices, there is one crucial area where he has none. He must earn a living, for himself and his family. *Must*. It strikes me what a dreadful weight that must be, a shoulder-pack he can never put down.

At The Howard, I am not sure I ever thought about my father's lot in life. Not like this. I only thought about how much I missed him. It was the same with my mother.

My father, William Johnson, descended from free upstate New Yorkers. "Upstate New York" is anywhere north of New York City. His father labored as a boatman. His mother, along with young William, worked in domestic service for a wealthy white family.

To my knowledge, my father did whatever he could to earn a living. I could imagine that if someone asked him his occupation, he might have said, "Whatever needs doing." In my restless imagination, I can feel the squeezing pressure of the relentless need to earn money. Before the orphanage and thereafter, money was always a problem in our home. We moved often. I cannot but wonder how this affected my father, what it might have done to his spirits. Did it deaden the spirit of the marriage?

My mother's lot was likely little different from many immigrant women of her era, especially Irish women. That she was born in England would not have allowed her a pass on her heritage. Catherine Cannon Qualter Johnson – Kate – arrived in the United States at the age of one. An early first marriage produced twelve children. Two achieved adulthood – out of twelve! So prior to marrying my father, she had known a life of childbirth and death. Her existence was one of constant loss and grief, of financial scarcity, if not want. Might her second marriage have seemed changeless – two more children, financial pressure, the necessity of constant moves?

Good, but hard. That is how I see a woman's lot. Thus far, all my children are alive and thriving, all five of them, a sixth on the way. (My mother would cross herself if I said this out loud.) All those years ago in The Howard, this is what I dreamed of, what I wished for. And yet, as each child birth has taken more out of me, I wonder how my mother survived. She must have been incredibly strong to do what had to be done.

On occasion, I have asked her how she did it, but she seemed to brush it aside. Maybe she saw my question as a passing curiosity rather than a desire to know.

"Oh, you just did what you had to do," she might say, something like that.

Well, some people do not. But she did. I suppose I could have pushed a bit, but out of respect for her, I chose not to.

Sometimes, when she worked, I would hear her hum Irish tunes. Especially if the task, darning socks or repairing a hem, allowed her to sit. "When Irish Eyes are Smiling" would bring a far-away look to her red-rimmed, tired-from squinting eyes. The same with "Too Ra Loo Ra Loo Ra." It was as if she was remembering something she had never known, something heart-felt even more than imagined. I am not sure she even knew the words. But the rhythms seemed to reach something deep within her that brushed her soul, unspoken, but there. Can there be such a thing as joyful sadness? That is what I saw in her, what I heard when the humming escaped.

Our lots in life, our fates. Most men and women seem to have little choice over *what*, only *how*. How you will go about it, your life, living it. Will you find a blessing in it or feel trapped? I find so many blessings in music, they overwhelm those rare moments when I feel caged.

My world was indeed "sheltered" and small. Most of those I knew lived in the same neighborhood and seldom traveled beyond. Family was the world to me, and more than ever, still is. Love and safety lay in its embrace. You could imagine a walled kingdom or a fenced-in prison, depending.

The key was acceptance. More than being accepted by my community, it appeared my own acceptance of my lot decided my happiness. Men and women, who did not take to their lots, often fell into drink or bottomless bitterness and despair.

I wonder how my parents adjusted. I try to imagine their lives as a mixed-race couple in a colored community. What drew them together? Attraction? Love? Or did their lots cast them up on a shore of common need? Even desperation? My mother, a widow trying to raise chidren with little means of support. My father, a working man, possibly lonely, almost 40 at marriage. Marrying a widow with two children, a white woman with all the judgments that likely followed. Judgments traveling in both directions.

I prefer to think it was decided by love.

When I was little, I did not ask them much. (I still do not press my mother, and I cannot with my father. He died a month before I turned seventeen, the same year I married.) Back then, the years at The Howard, children did not press adults for information not freely given. Besides, I was focused on visits from them, on seeing them, on home. On just being with them. John Henry and I wanted them happy to see us.

As I mentioned earlier, they rarely came to The Howard. With work and the tight-collar orphanage rules for visitors, how could they? Although disappointment sometimes overwhelmed me, age has helped me understand what a hardship it must have been for them. I cannot be sure, but I continue to suspect discomfort traveling outside of Weeksville was part of it.

Remember Frances? The girl at The Howard, whose anger had no eyes, blindly splattering hatefulness? She would say things to me like "Maybe they don't want to come, see their precious princess. Maybe they got better things to do."

It was as if she was trying to plant a seed of doubt. I refused to water it with tears. Instead, I would thumb through things I could have said in return. "At least someone comes to see me" or "at least I have someone."

I took satisfaction in the thoughts, but never said them. They were cruel. I would try to think, "I am not Frances. I am glad I am not Frances." I would think it over and over again, chanting it to myself until it settled me like a prayer. But what little sympathy I had for Frances vanished like spilled water through cracks between floorboards.

My parents never did offer much in the way of their pasts. In time, I came to understand they put their energy into *doing*. There was little left over for backward glances or gaiety.

Later, graced with children, I made up my mind to find time for them among all my tasks. I am not passing judgment on my parents. They did what they thought they had to do. But with my children, there would be a game here, a magic trick there, songs in between. They would know they were loved and not just something that I had to be responsible for. And lo, their laughing delight lifts me in turn.

Chapter Fifteen: John Henry

His death left a hole in my life, one that can never be filled. John Henry, my brother. My only sibling from my parents' marriage. Two half-sisters from my mother's first marriage were too far removed from my life to ever be a part of it. We were related even less in deed than in blood.

John Henry, gone at nineteen. So many unanswered questions, now unanswerable. He died at the Kosciusko Elevated Station, hit by a train. It left me shaken to the tips of my roots, my sheltered life laid open. I grieved so hard, I wondered if my insides might turn out. It frightened my husband, who tried to console me. Though there were many possible explanations, there were no answers. I could find no clear way to close the final chapter of his too short life.

In my darkest hours, questions buzzed my brain like mocking birds protecting a nest. Had he been drinking and fallen in front of the train? Was he pushed? Was it a mugging? A robbery? Was it revenge for a debt unpaid? Was it racial? Could it have been tied in with a woman? Handsome as he was, girls and women were keen on John Henry.

Or, as the police claimed, was it suicide? There were witnesses, including the train conductor, who said he jumped.

The police never exactly fall all over themselves trying to solve the death of a colored man. If he was invisible to them in life, why would it be different in death? That sounds angry to me, as if I am trying to blame someone or something for his death. I have nothing else to go on, and that is part of my hair-tearing grief.

When I reach a point like this, I have to stop, or at least, step back. To continue in that way would be to risk drowning in my sadness and regret.

For me, it will remain a life that did not happen. I wonder, did I fail him? My official responsibilities at The Howard were schooling and training. But I was also supposed to keep an eye on John Henry – which I did. After we returned to Brooklyn and finished our schooling at PS 28, however, our lives parted. Direction found us. Did I become so caught up in mine that I forgot about his? I feel sick when I think about it.

Life was never exactly the berries for him, and I am not sure why. He was very close to our mother. In fact, he had a tattoo on his right forearm that said "Mother." Was she in some way a burden to him? In their closeness, was he weighed down by her needs, by what she expected of him? I do not like thinking this way, but again, I am left only with questions.

A handsome boy, John Henry was an even more handsome man. He was searching for his place in the world when he enlisted in the Navy. We celebrated a "Bell Bottom" in the family. Yet just three months later, in April of 1924, he was discharged, honorably to our knowledge. Barely five days later, he passed. At first, my thoughts swooped to and fro, like a bat at dusk, searching, *searching*, for an answer. I was desperate to know what happened. I believe I am fated to think like this forever, wondering, wondering about all the "what ifs."

He was so gay at his enrollment, thinking maybe his search had ended. He had found his place in the order of things. *Again*, what happened? We hear colored men on ships work as cooks and waiters who serve officers. They do all this scut work, the dirtiest, greasiest and most dangerous jobs, including handling munitions. But John Henry was to train as a fireman, a skilled position with employment potential after the Navy.

My mind churned harder than the butter we made at The Howard. Did reality burst his dream, giving him second thoughts? Did someone break the contract? Did he discover he was there to be a waiter? Did he realize that working as a domestic or stevedore lacked the upward path he had been promised, that it would be no different for a colored seaman than in civilian life? I do not know. *I do not know*.

His passing left me wondering at the burden colored men bear. Much as they might wish to, they cannot avoid going out into the wider world, not ultimately. In *our* world, women can marry, maybe remain at home, but men *have* to go out. They have to find work, leaving them exposed to the white race and that unthinking emotion, *hatred*.

What did he find in that world, in the military world? White uniforms and black thoughts? Traditions left over from the time of slavery? It was a world of separation. When the races came together, they were together only physically. It was white man up, colored man down. Same country, different navies. Did John Henry feel this too intensely? Did it flare from simmer to quick boil, leaving him with no way to quiet the sting?

There I go again. Distressed. Upset. Searching in vain for answers. Beneath it all, I am seething. His death has introduced me to emotions I scarcely recognize. They frighten me. And it is because I can never know, even as my mind continues to shout questions.

I dream of him often, think of him every day. I wonder how his passing has affected our mother. (Thank God our father was spared the loss of his son.) I believe it has affected her mightily, has damaged her like a wound that will not heal. A child of hers had survived to adulthood, developed a personality, a presence, a relationship beyond diapers. She was two-minds/one-heart close to him, leaned on him, depended on him.

She began to deteriorate after that, aging rapidly, her health problems worsening. It was as if a steadfast will, that had allowed her to weather so much loss, finally surrendered. This was the back-breaking straw, her last son.

Did it draw a dark curtain over the future for our mother, blotting out hope's faint light? It was as if she could no longer find a way to tomorrow or count on anything. But I also believe it had to do with John Henry. I believe he owned a special place in her heart. Something about him lifted my brother slightly above the love she bore for all her children. She has hinted at a desire to be with him in death, as close as in life.

It got me thinking about sons and daughters, and where they stood in relation to their mothers. Where they stand. My son, John, whom we call "Dukie", the oldest of my children, is the only boy to date. He is special in that he was the first. (Special also in that he lives apart. from me with his grandparents. Maybe I will talk about that, later.) But is there something in me that sets him aside from, or above, his sisters? If there is, I do not see it. I respond to Catherine, Dorothy, Irene and Thelma as I do Dukie – by who they are. I love them all, but I cannot treat them the same. Their personalities will not permit it.

This is not a judgment of my mother. I am just speaking of how I sense my life compared to what I know of hers. She has had a hard life, much harder than mine, with enough grief to stop a runaway train. And she came from a different world with different customs and expectations.

In her time, a mother looked to sons for financial support if her husband died, unless a daughter had married well, sometimes even if a daughter married well.

I now know our mother depended on John Henry for support after our father passed – more than I ever realized. My gosh, my brother was only 16! I cannot help, but wonder how much of a burden that must have been for him. Heaven knows, he labored to carry it, worked at any job he could find.

To enlist in the Navy, he must have had her support. Perhaps a portion of his pay was to go to her or to an allotment for enlisting that she never received. Did the Navy recruiter promise something? Was she led to believe there would be something to boost her meager finances until her son completed his training? When that money was not forthcoming, did our mother press him to seek his release?

It appeared this was the case, as we later learned, and he was granted a release based on witnessed letters that he was her sole means of support. But that was only a paper explanation, a means to satisfy a record keeper. It did not begin to examine the weight of disappointment that likely crushed my brother's spirit. Again, what a burden for a 19 year old!

Wherever the truth, at the beginning of his adult life, a possible career in front of him, it ended. I cannot bear to imagine the impact it had upon John Henry to lose out on his Navy career. I think of an airplane launching flight only to return to the runway shortly upon take-off. Or worse, crashing. I do suspect the answer I can never know lies in there somewhere.

I also cannot bear to think harshly of our mother. Barely above the surface of poverty in marriage, widowhood pushed her further down. But I have wondered if Irish mothers were tied by custom to their sons in particular. I would wonder what a son represented. Was he a means of keeping a loving connection to a deceased husband? Or maybe an imagined perfection against a tainted memory? A bit of both? Or was he someone to desperately cling to even if it meant surrendering a chance at his own life?

John Henry is buried at the National Military

Cemetery on Jamaica Avenue, near the Brooklyn / Queens border. With lead-weighted regret, I think of all he never knew, and never would know.

Following a sudden death, the living are left with all those questions that will remain unanswered. Look at me, forever guessing, wondering, until I have to close their presence in my mind. I have children to attend to. And they, my children, *will* know him. They already recognize "Uncle Johnny" by the picture I keep close at hand. The only image I keep closer is the picture of him I hold in my heart.

Chapter Sixteen: What Makes Me, *Me*?

I find myself thinking more to the point these days, not wandering as far. Likely not a surprise with young children and babies to care for. Thinking is my outlet, my recreation. It is as if I am forever going through a library sorting and re-sorting the books. Many of the thoughts of my journey through life remain unspoken.

To some, that might seem odd, even funny. "Journey?" they might say. "Horsefeathers! What journey? She is only twenty-six years old. Her *journey* is just beginning. Sounds like she might have a little too much Sarah Bernhardt in her. Well, give it time. Life will straighten her out on that account. Give her something to really fret about."

Maybe it is true, maybe I see drama where there is none. But I am not imagining what happened. Born to a mixed-race couple, there were times when I was an object of curiosity. People stared, not seldom boldly. My mother's life was forever taxed with spirit-crushing loss. I will always wonder what that took from her, what parts of her I can never know.

I was separated from my parents between four and twelve, living in the orphanage. Kings Park, as lovely as it was, felt like another country. The orphanage ended tragically in 1918. Although I was gone, back living in Brooklyn, I am still haunted by the suffering at the end. Two children lost their feet to frostbite. But by chance, it could have been me. I cannot bear to try to imagine living without feet.

I grew up through The Great War, ill at ease, wondering if it might come to America. I survived the Spanish Influenza of 1918 that took so many from this Earth.

When I was sixteen, my father passed. Then four years later, John Henry in that "accident." I had not turned twenty-one.

Through it all, I am reminded everyday what it means to be a person of color in America. Like a nagging cough, it never quite goes away.

I can be blissfully singing "I'm Always Chasing Rainbows," a song that grants me feelings of hope. All of a sudden, there it is. Maybe "rainbows" set off thoughts of color and a downward-looping chain starts. I could be passing from church on a Sunday draped in sunlight, filled with a joyful spirit. An automobile might go by, white passengers staring at me as they might a creature in a zoo. My joy collapses like a circus tent after the center pole has been removed. In the midst of happiness, doubt.

It is not my problem, but it will always be *a* problem for me. I can look in a mirror and be grateful for what I see. The image does not disturb me, is not the source of doubt and misgivings. It is what I see in the eyes of a white person that leaves me confused. Those eyes, widening, then quickly narrowing, reflect uncertainty, fear and sometimes distaste. Occasionally, I will also detect hunger in a white man that has nothing to do with me as a person. Place him with his own kind, the poorly concealed hunger would give way to race.

I know what it is, and then, when I think about it a little longer, I do not. At times, I feel I have a handle on understanding. Then suddenly, on the wings of a fleeting thought, comprehension deserts me. It leaves me dizzy, grasping to right myself, feeling an invisible crow is pecking at my hope. I *will not* give in, tempted to surrender to thoughts darker than an undertaker's parlor, but they are there. Imagine knowing you will have to live your life like this.

This is what gave birth to the *drama*. It leaves me wondering how I survived. What was it that protected me from all that might have taken me down? What allowed me to push on? What made the difference? What made me, *me*?

Part of it, I would think, has to be *patience*. Put me on a line, I just settle in until it moves. A quality not rare for a colored person, I have always been patient. It was in me, but it was also necessary. Had I allowed myself to become impatient – wanting to be home with my parents – I might have panicked.

Notice I said "allowed myself." That suggests (to me, at least) that patience is a way of being under control. It is more than something that just lies within. It is something that can be added to or subtracted from. The math is up to us.

Another part would be *tolerance*. While it would be hard to have tolerance without patience, they are not the same.

One might say, "Do not be taking special credit for 'tolerance.'" In turn, I would say, "When was a colored person ever permitted to be intolerant?" Say what one might, I still believe that tolerance is a part of what makes me, *me*.

When I encounter intolerance, even when I just think about it, it leaves me confused. Well, more than confused. Confused and amused all in one. At least, that is what I am trying to say. Kind of like I laugh at the ignorance and wonder at what could have been at the same time.

The conflict in these thoughts is never greater than when I am in church listening to the sermon. I do not just nod my head and agree with what is said. When my father-in-law preaches, I listen. I think about it, about intolerance outside and even within the church. Questions batter me about faith as professed or practiced. Not infrequently, his words call forth my questions which in turn drown his words out.

I think that anyone can find a church. But do they find one that tells them what they want to hear or teaches them what they need to know? Sometimes, it can seem to be about pleasing members rather than showing them a way.

I have wondered how Reverend Hamlin, once he embraced his faith, managed to hold on to it. Surely, it must have been tested by the intolerance he has found in this world. I suspect the answer lies in "keeping the faith." Once committed, you dedicate yourself to preserving it regardless of what life throws at you.

I know that is true for me. In questioning God's will, it reveals to me I have faith no matter how it is tested. I frequently wonder why God has allowed us to drift so far from what must have been

His original plan. Why has He not done something to correct it? Leaving it to His creations does not seem to work as well as it could.

Oddly, I find such joy in church, I wonder how, after calling people together, it fails to keep them together. How is it that people briefly united in spirit, so quickly pull apart when they leave church? Perhaps they remember they have to plunge back into the same world as before the service. Maybe the joy is just enough to help them hold steady with what they struggle to tolerate each week.

As I said, tolerance lies within me, but I believe Sundays in church help to strengthen it. I believe that is as it should be. A church has to stand against intolerance in any form. We must speak out when other groups preach exclusion, even if the group is another church. On occasion, I will read about some church declaring a group of people "evil" who are just different. If there is anything more un-Christ-like than that, I do not know what it is.

I just feel so blessed that tolerance is a part of my nature. I do not have to grope for it in the dark or remember to take it with me when I leave home. And when I think of myself as blessed, I receive it as another sign of my faith.

My son, Dukie, visited us today. He played outside with his sister, Catherine. My two oldest, I could hear them. Sounded like he was pulling her in the wagon. Whatever it was, I could hear her telling him how to do it "right." The next two were supposed to be taking a nap. Only one was, my fourth child, Irene. The third, Dorothy, chose to lie with her head in my lap while I fed Thelma, the baby.

I pretended that I did not know Dorothy was there. And she pretended not to notice me combing her hair with my fingers, caressing her face. She is a sweet child with a wandering eye, what the doctors call a "strabismus." Her presence brought me back to thoughts of what made me the person I am.

I caught myself smiling at Dorothy. Thoughts of my children will do that, and there, *right there*, was another part of me revealed. The smile in front of the laughter, the eternal song in my heart. I have said it before, I know. Dewy-eyed? Probably. I am very sentimental. But to acknowledge song and laughter is to acknowledge me. I cannot imagine life without them, do not want to.

I am always humming. Like songbirds when morning sun touches their feathers, I will break into song for the sheer joy of it. "My Wild Irish Rose." My mother likes it. "You Made Me Love You." It makes me think of my husband, John, a mail-sorter at the Post Office. "You made me love you, I didn't want to do it...." I did want to do it, and I do. Always will.

I heard a recording of the "St. Louis Blues." Cannot get that music out of my head. Do not want to. I will hum it in a private moment, but not around my children. I might break into song, and I do not feel the words are fit for their young ears. Besides, the sentiments do not reflect my feelings or my life. But, oh, I do love that music!

Music aside – well, with me that is not possible. But for a moment, music aside, I am fortunate that hatred and bitterness cannot find lodging in my soul. I will not permit my darker emotions to root in my thinking, no matter how hard they try. It can be hard to do. I believe you can only do it if you never stop doing it. If you do, you have given up or are in the final steps of surrender. It leaves me feeling like a little mountain that cannot be climbed. Among more majestic peaks, I am scarcely noticed, but I am there. I like that feeling.

I believe one part, above all, has protected me through life, and allowed me to be me. I have been blessed with a capacity to love. I take no credit for it. I regard it as a gift for it has always been there. It allows me to overcome hurt feelings and the dark thoughts that gather around those feelings like moths swarming a nightlight.

I feel the love most when I am in church, surrounded by my family. My senses fill with the physical world about me, and I lift. I smell wood and wood polish, the perfumes, lotions and talcum of tight-pressed bodies. Closer to me, I smell the sweet breath of little children, *my* children.

I see flowers stacked in vases, and I warm imagining the bouquet. Above my head, sunlight streams through stained glass, its intricate construction revealed. I take in the women in their Sunday finery, adorned as if they were attending a ball. Rainbow colors – peach, lemon yellow, a pink that shimmers – jubilate among the somber blacks, browns and grays. Some of the women are aglow in white, their skin radiant from an inner happiness.

I hear the words of the sermon reaching for my mind, often detouring to my heart. They march in a rhythm set by my father-in-law. His voice released from his otherwise reserved personality, the words arrive like music. Battle music perhaps, but music all the same.

Music. Throughout the service, above it all, there is the music – the choir, the piano, the congregation. No wall can contain the heavenly spine-tingling harmonies. The hair on the back of my neck and my soul lift with fountains of music. Were it not for my children, my voice would be among those in the choir. As it is, I join them from the pew. I gently nudge my children to lift their voices, whether they know the words or not. Pit music against words, music will win.

In the midst of it all, I overflow with love.

Chapter Seventeen: Buttons

Yesterday was a button-sewing day. I had put it off long enough. I tend to do that with darning socks as well. I do not mind doing either, but they tend to be low on my to-do list. Easier to not notice for a while.

I learned these skills at The Howard, though I imagine eventually my mother would have taught me. So much of what I do now, I learned there. I am grateful for that. I need to say that, to remind myself of my gratitude because I never wanted to be there. That has not changed.

Buttons. I was speaking of buttons. I have a small button box. I keep it next to my needle case, the spools of thread a rainbow of colors. When I need to select a button, I tend to spill them on a white cloth or pillow case. You might think it would be easy, then, to select the color I am searching for. Not so. The colors can change, depending upon the materials around them. Black is not always so black, and white can take on colors laid close to it. Brown and ivory lighten or darken, depending on how they are nested.

In the house, under yellow light, I struggle to separate white from bone or ivory. Sometimes, to trust my judgment, I have to take it out into daylight. Even that might fool me, depending on whether it is a sun-filled or cloudy day. It is the same with black, brown and deep garnet. Heaven help me if I lay them out on anything other than white. Place them against a pattern, and I am lost.

The problem is even worse matching thread to a sock toe or a tear in a dress. The colors blend, disappearing or popping out, again depending upon what is around them. Sometimes, I lean against a windowpane squinting until my eyes blur, and still end up with a mismatch.

On occasion, I might say to myself, "Oh, hell's bells. No one will ever notice. Just grab a button." And it is true. You do not. Even if at first you do, after a while, you do not – notice. The button? The thread? They have become part of the fabric.

It is only when you separate them, see them set apart, that you notice them more. How often does that happen in this world? There is always a background to something – or someone. And when I say "someone," it is obvious what I am getting at, is it not? I knew it from the moment I noticed buttons changing color.

I believe that separation can only happen in the mind, can only happen *if* the mind permits it. It only happens if the mind decides that is the way it wants to hold onto something. It must ignore everything that surrounds the separating.

Race. It is like an underground river that flows forgotten much of the time. But every so often, after a sudden rain, it gushes out of the ground. Roaring wildly, it swamps most everything in its way. And when it passes, it leaves devastation and death behind.

We have this need to name things. Scientists do it. They sort out to understand. When they do this with people, they separate us. Why? We already have a name. *People*. We are all people, human beings. When we separate people by names, do we unintentionally encourage them to see the differences? Do they then become blind to what they share in common? I think so.

Consider my brother John Henry and me. Our father was black, our mother white. But our father was also referred to as "Colored" or "Negro." It was as if a search grasped for a name that did not quite satisfy. My mother was still "White." Apparently, that was enough.

Looking at an old picture of John Henry, I see a dark-skinned boy with white facial features. Actually, that was a problem with the picture; he was light-skinned enough to pass for white. He did when he enrolled in the Navy. My pictures suggest someone plunked in the middle between races, my skin slightly darker than my brother's. These facts did not matter, still do not. Remember my math? When the sorters finished with us, we were both "Colored."

Please do not misunderstand me. This is not a complaint. Call me what you will, I am still *me*. I believe the name changes more how *you* see me, than it changes me. It robs you of how you could see me.

I do believe, however, that people of color will never be comfortable with any name that separates us. Invented by a white person or a colored person reacting to white people, it does not satisfy the search. All it does is remind us who we are, something we already know.

Colored. Negro. Black. African. Somewhere,

I once heard the word, "*Hottentot*." *The black race.*
Fill in the blank. But if it is filled in by a white
person, then it is not us. It is what someone-not-us
has chosen to call us. I do not accept that. However I
choose to think of myself will always be my decision.
I will never grant it to someone else. When I think of
who I am, race is but a teaspoon among the measures
I use.

I am not speaking of words used to belittle
another or worse. Those words refer only to
themselves and those who utter them. No, I am
speaking of honest if misbegotten attempts to sort
and clarify. To *name*.

Imagine if I were to refer to all white people
as "Pinkies" because some have a pink tinge? (I am
smiling as I write this, but I had to pick something.)
Would that likely be accepted with all the shadings
that fall under "white?" I believe the reaction would
be akin to including all shadings of people of color
as "black." Convenient perhaps, but for whom?

I believe it important to think about what you
say, especially if you are about to say it of another
person. Or of something you know little about. I
think it also important you not only select words with
care, but that you control your voice as well. If not,
your words may take on unintended meaning – a
second caboose dragging on a train.

I speak softly. I know that because people
have told me. The only time I raise my voice is in
song. I do not believe in raising my voice to get a
message across. When people do that, I sense they
are feeling threatened. If so, they are surrendering to
emotion – fear, anger or both. If they are hoping to

convince someone of something, they are already losing the battle. The louder they get, the harder it is to become the listener they want.

When you tell someone "to be quiet," you are telling them, 'I am right, you are wrong." It is even worse when a person is told to "shut up." I do *not* like that expression. It is like a slap across the face.

I remember another expression, "Speak softly but carry a big stick." Or maybe it was "Speak softly *and* carry a big stick." Whichever, I think I read it in a school history lesson. President Teddy Roosevelt said it. He was president when I saw first light. Anyway, I do not carry a big stick, do not plan to. If I did, I might find an excuse to use it.

I believe I understand what he meant. He was speaking of our country, of strength behind humility. Perhaps that is necessary for a nation among other nations. But from what I read of Mr. Roosevelt, he did not strike me as a humble man. Nor did he speak softly. Would he then have been more likely to use that big stick at troubled times? If something angered him or left him fearful, unsure of himself? This appears to be the case. He did not follow his own advice.

This expression between people concerns me. I think it increases the likelihood of disturbance between neighbors because at its core, it seems less than honest. You act calm, but underneath, you do not trust. Why? Are you afraid? If you are afraid, does your voice try to hide it? If so, how? By speaking louder? If you speak louder, does the tone warn the other you are reaching for your big stick?

Distrust will probably lead to distrust. Then

the other person – or country – will likely look for a bigger stick.

I think you need to speak softly, but know what you are speaking about. If not, you need to listen and say little until you have something helpful to say. If you speak softly and others speak louder, might it not be better to continue to speak softly? Maybe they will calm. But even if they do not, I do not want them pushing me into something I am not. I do not want to become a person I do not wish to be. Is that not what we try to teach our children? I do.

I speak softly because that is who I am. I am a button that will blend with any material. I am one of the threads that will anchor that button securely. Again, you might not notice me, but I am there.

Chapter Eighteen: Time

The Howard prepared me for what I do. As a married woman with children, I would say they prepared me well. After the move to Kings Park in 1911, its full name became The Howard Orphanage and Industrial School. It was there I learned to use time with industry. I did not waste it, nor do I now. You will never catch me fiddling while Rome burns. Okay, maybe humming a bit, but I will likely be busy.

What I just wrote might come across as lacking in modesty. If so, I would be taking credit unearned. My way with time was born of need. At The Howard, it was necessary to use time well. Now, with five children, a sixth on the way, it is more necessary than ever. You either use the time you are granted or let it slip by. Either way, it is gone forever. There will be no second chance. I believe I somehow managed to grasp that somewhere around twelve – again, that time of change.

They preached it to us often enough in daily lessons and Sunday sermons. *"Tempus fugit."* How many times did I hear that? Time flies. Turned out, it was true, could not have been truer.

Somewhere, through it all, the lesson sunk in and rooted. I can feel it lurking in my mind when I wake up in the morning. It almost hums like an idling motor awaiting gear mesh. My thoughts begin to turn over as if an invisible hand is cranking them. It serves nothing to lie abed for an extra five or ten minutes. My fingers will begin to twitch, then my toes, my body readying for activity. I get up and get to it.

At the outset of each day, I often find myself humming "Lift Every Voice and Sing." It lofts me above the Earthly sleep clinging to my eyes. Mr. James Weldon Johnson's words, his brother John's music, put me in the right frame of mind. *My* gears mesh, and I am ready for the day.

The song is as beautiful as any hymn we sing in church. There is something holy in the sound, a prayer sung aloud. I remember some of the lines, but a few remain fuzzy. Why is that? The first line – "Lift every voice and sing, till earth and Heaven ring" – carries me to the ethers. There, I am borne away.

One day, I plan to memorize the words. In my Sunday prayers, I always recite the line, "Keep us forever in the path, we pray." It helps me approach the coming week renewed, ready to pour love into what I do.

What I do has purpose, but I take no credit for that, either. Children to tend, I have to have a plan or time would laugh and run away from me. My plan may be no more than a good intention, but it is enough to get me started. I can build on it as I go.

I might be bathing Irene and Thelma in the claw tub. Soap bubbles, Lysol disinfectant and scrubbed baby skin scent the air. Dorothy will be close by, likely just over my shoulder. She will usually want to chat. Lately, she has been tossing an old, scuffed-up, rubber handball, learning how to catch it. Sometimes, the ball will bounce into the tub or even off my head. Either will set her two younger sisters laughing, playing, splashing. Then they will want her to keep doing it, turning it into a game. And there I am, trying to complete a task, so I can move on to the next.

I decided, the day Dukie was born, the best way was to get to the task, but add a little fun. Often, it might seem spontaneous, and sometimes it is. But behind it lies my intention to reach for happiness when and where I can.

With five children now, my plan, by need as much as desire, is to spread attention. In the end, I have no problem with the splashing. Heaven knows, I caused much of it. On my knees, I will lean against a towel draped over the curved edge of the tub. A washcloth in one hand, scrubbing the girls, I will reach behind and tickle Dorothy with the other. Soon the bathroom explodes with squeals of delight, mine included.

The water? I can mop that up later with an old towel. Either way, I will be tired, but the kids are happy. It is a better way for them, better for me, too.

Later that morning, I take that weariness to my bath. Warm water is a pleasure I allow myself each day *after* the children are bathed and dressed. The rule: The older children play with the younger and keep an eye on them. No one goes outside to play until Mama has her bath.

The bath is a rare private time, to think or not. Soaking in warm water draws vigor through my body and weariness from it. Afloat in the warmth, I will remember the line, "Keep us forever in the path, we pray." I will carry that fragment of prayer through the day. At night, I recite it in bed, my spirit restored before sleep can do the same for my body.

Private time. I believe everyone needs a bit of it to count on each day. I do. It is not that I want to escape my life. That private moment is part of it. If anything, it helps me move toward what I have to do, refreshed, stronger, looking forward to it. Looking forward.

At The Howard, there was no privacy. There was no money for curtains nor was there room to spare for partitions. Everything was communal. *Everything*! I learned to manage the lack of privacy, but I never lost the desire for it.

My sole memory of privacy is my bed, beneath the covers. This was never more true than 1915 when I turned twelve and began to change. Several of the girls, including me, began to dress or undress in bed, under a sheet. It was harder to do that way, but that was what we did as the familiar slowly vanished.

I remember seeing a girl do this a year or two earlier. It seemed odd to me, almost funny seeing her squirm beneath her tented sheet. In 1915, I understood.

In many ways, The Howard is the reason my mind became the inner chamber of my privacy. Though it is probably true for everyone, I know it was the case for me.

Sometimes, I think I live two lives, the one I live on the outside and the one in my mind. They exist together, but they are not the same. In one, I do what I have to do. The other, I think about what I could do if the world were different. Think about what I *would* do.

But hand-in-hand, my two lives taken together are good. The life in my mind helps me live the other each day. It is where the songs come from. If a day darkens, I can enter my mind, rest a bit, and figure out where the light is hiding. Once I find it, and I always do, then it is "up and at 'em."

A recent dark spell, *Prohibition*, has led me to worry some about my children. It brought bootleg liquor and crime to our neighborhood. Why should I expect otherwise? As I understand it, it is everywhere. I see men returning home, lunch pails filled with beer, see people openly involved in "the trade." I probably even know a few without realizing it.

I worry about how it could affect the lives of my children now, but even more, later. There will come a time when they will no longer be under my protection. John and I will have to trust in what we taught them, but I fear the uncontrollable. With crime about, things can sometimes happen to the innocent caught up with the guilty.

My curiosity got the better of me recently. I asked a young man in our congregation how bad it was in our neighborhood, Prohibition crime.

He rolled his eyes, caught himself and said, "You mean the gin mills? Sorry Miz Hamlin, but comes to hooch, I don't know from nothing."

Those few words carried an earful. I decided from then on to keep my curiosity to myself.

Privacy and my children. If you have one, you are not going to have the other, not at the same moment. And why would anyone expect that? Children are just doing what they are supposed to be doing, being children. I have the great, God-given gift of my mind to draw from while helping them discover theirs. What a full-of-wonder responsibility!

I sometimes wonder, am I just getting older or is each birth taking more out of me? Whichever or both, my children make my life what it is. Make it better and busier. I am not sure which is more, but it is a good problem to have. Either way, it is still better.

Chapter Nineteen: A Link in the Chain

When I was a young girl – I think I was eight – I heard about the sinking of the Titanic. We all did at The Howard. I am sure I will always remember where I was when I heard about it. I remember where I was when I heard John Henry died.

For a while, the thought of the Titanic buzzed like an electric wire, enough to make your nerves jump. Sometimes we would see an old newspaper with a drawing of the sinking an artist imagined. To me, it seemed real. It gave me bad dreams. Though the dreams faded in time, they never completely disappeared.

The thoughts of harsh, violent deaths too grim to imagine, still haunt me from time to time. The vast floating party ending so ghastly, people dying in frigid waters, knowing they were about to die. It was the stuff of nightmares.

The floating party. Night after night, celebrating as if it could never end. But celebrating what? Exactly what is it that the wealthy celebrate? Their wealth? Maybe, but I am not so sure. Freedom? Freedom from what? Freedom to do what? Do they have even a tad more freedom than I? If so, I am unable to see what it is. Fun? Possibly. They seem to have more idle time on their hands than I. It would appear they try to fill it with fun. But is it fun? Or do they celebrate in order not to think about time? To forget its passage. Time may be the only thing their wealth cannot buy.

With Prohibition now, it feels like the same thing, only worse, though I know not why. We read of endless parties in the newspaper. We see pictures of wild celebrations, of police raids on speakeasies. Barrels of beer and spirits are split open and spilled in the streets. We hear of tales of corruption. The police may be among the celebrants at one of hundreds of parties all over the city. Articles speak of "good times." Are they? And the parties? To what end? Fun? Back to fun again. Escape? Is it? Like on the Titanic?

I think of all those people "celebrating" God only knows, doing anything to escape their lives. Doing everything they can to temporarily forget. While they seek to escape their homes through rivers of alcohol, orphans are desperate to find one.

I do not want to forget; I want to remember. Remember the sparkle of joy-filled eyes when The Quartette sang, but also the blackened soles of frostbitten feet. Remember the relief of a pay envelope with enough to get by, and the fear of the lights cut off next month. Remember Dorothy's smile as she healed from tonsillitis, but also the terror of croup. Each child-breath becomes a gasping stretch for merciful air.

If I am to continue teaching my children, I need to recall what I have learned. I want to teach them how to move toward the world, not escape it. And I want them to do it guided by their consciences, moral in what they do. My husband and I want them legal in their actions, not seeking the unlawful for a thrill.

In the newspaper, women, just as they were when they sailed on the Titanic, are dressed to the nines. Gowns, furs, and jewels glittered like stars. The men spiffy in tuxedos. To go out drinking? It seems so empty. But they seem so happy, acting as if it could go on forever, their faces so radiant. Radiant from alcohol? You could almost smell it rising from the page.

The partying has been going on since the end of The Great War. For a while, I wondered what President Hoover thought of it all. He seems so separated from everyday people, I suspect he does not think about it at all.

"How could he?" John said. "Man's focus is divided between his picture in tomorrow's paper and the next course in tonight's dinner."

Maybe a bit unfair, but I laughed. It was a nice break from the worrisome partying going on around us.

All around the revelers are those who keep doing what has to be done while they celebrate. I re-read that last line, and realize it might sound like I am judging the revelers. I just wish the newspapers would photograph the janitor who has to clean up their mess afterward. Maybe a columnist could write about the street-sweeper who clears the gutter of their trash. I am speaking of the unnoticed people who spark the city, making it work. Some call them the "working stiffs." Said in the right tone, it sounds respectful. I hope so. I see myself as one of them.

We are out here working, caring for our homes, our children, quietly celebrating life through rightful living. If there is a right way to live, we are doing it. Living this way, we are not aware that we are "celebrating" even when we are. Celebrating something real, something you can touch as sure as the uplifted brow of a loving child.

In the morning I am greeted by smiling faces rather than a hangover. I come into the day with my heart open rather than my eyes shut. I want to move toward, rather than away from, light. I celebrate Sundays, rather than clinging to the commode, trying to escape too much Saturday night.

I was seventeen when I married John Francis Hamlin. For a brief period, I worked in a wig factory. I started sometime after I turned sixteen, stopping before the birth of Dukie, and returning afterward. We needed the money.

When my work would come up in conversation, people would look surprised. A few even laughed. I know, wigs? In the twentieth century? Did they not disappear more than a hundred years ago in America? To some, it probably sounded frivolous. For me, it was a job, a paying job, important at that point in my life.

At work, I learned that we sold wholesale to wig shops and department stores. I began to study the base of our customers and the worth of our work. Beyond the theatrical wigs, our primary customers were older colored women and female Hasidim. I believe the colored women were beyond the days of burned scalps. No more straightening their hair with Congolene or marcelling it with hot irons. No matter the process or product, it was all lye – a lie (I know) sold to colored women.

The Hasidic Jewish women were following

strict religious custom that required a covered head in public. Although their heads were shaved at marriage, the majority, to my limited knowledge, grew their hair back. Tucked under those wigs, it must have been intolerable on broiling July and August Brooklyn days.

In the end, I was able to view my work as a contribution. That was important to me, also. I regarded myself as one who does what has to be done while others swirl through the night seeking forgetfulness.

I think I developed that way of thinking during my years at The Howard singing for alms. It was referred to as "fundraising," seeking donations wherever they might be found. Call it as you please, it was begging. If you were too proud, you were in trouble.

Looking back, I believe I was proud, but not too. At the time, I never thought about myself that way, so how could I know? My mind was set on contributing, on doing what I could to make things better. Better for everyone. It is what little children do if you give them a purpose and a bit of praise.

When I sang with The Quartette, they used to take photographs of us for handbills. They would post them in the neighborhood around the building where we were supposed to sing in Brooklyn. Usually it was a church. On Long Island, they would post the handbills in the closest towns – Kings Park, Smithtown, St. James, possibly Northport.

I once heard a photographer say, "Dress 'em up, trot 'em out and line 'em up."

We would powder ourselves and don our

frilled white dresses. Someone, a female chaperone, would usually dab a drop of perfume behind our ears. Then out we would go, and *poof!* another picture.

We understood it, accepted it. I did. As I have said, it was my way. I wanted people around me to be happy. But there was the attention, too, the praise. I cannot deny that it was fun.

I might hear a voice say, "Ooh! You sing like little angels."

I might see a smiling face with tarnished teeth surrounded by thin pale lips above a bay window. I would look long enough to drop a curtsy. Then I would look away to enjoy the words without having to decipher their sincerity. Again, as a child, I wanted to take everything for what it seemed to be.

Children in an orphanage, probably any institution, are starving for praise. But there is a caution hidden in it. Its golden-white radiance can light up your spirit or blind you, maybe both. Even delivered sincerely, it can fool you into thinking it could go on forever. You might come to think of life as an endless performance, a silvered chain of parties.

But it can end, all of it, like the Titanic. Even something massive and strong can be as fragile as a Dresden tea cup or a newborn baby. Look at The Howard. *The Howard Colored Orphanage and Industrial School.* I write it that way to remember it. All those years, all the work, the constant soul-scorching fundraisers, all those hopes, *gone.* Gone because of one broken link in that chain.

Chapter Twenty: The Memories Insist

Yesterday, I was up early. No surprise with young children, I always rise early. It is necessary to take command of the day. For a few moments, I just sat in the glory of silence even as I shivered awake. One of these days, I need to replace this terrycloth robe, thinned from too many washings. Bright white when I bought it, the robe has faded to tabby-streaked gray.

Before I lit the coal stove, I pushed back the curtain over the kitchen window. After The Howard, I just had to have curtains. The sun was beginning to break over the roofs of the houses behind us. Slanting golden against the top of our building, it would be an hour before its warmth reached us, and then, only for a little while.

I lit the stove and sat huddled at the kitchen table, watching the moisture on the stove. Beaded up from the previous night, it slowly vanished with the rising heat. That is when I put the kettle on to heat water for tea and oatmeal.

I sat with my arms tightly folded, awaiting warmth from up-curling steam and the radiant stove. Before he left for the Post Office, my husband stoked the coal furnace, banked the night before. The super is supposed to do that, but sometimes he sleeps late. It takes a while for the house to warm. At the table, I gathered my wits, listening to the house "waking." The pipes groaned and the frame wood cracked from slow-rising heat.

Images of country life, of Kings Park, of The Howard flickered like moving pictures in my mind. I found myself comparing life there with my life now in Brooklyn, the country with the city.

I think the coolness of the morning had something to do with it. I love autumn, but at the orphanage, cooler days reminded you wind-driven, muscle-stiffening cold was coming. Months of frost-nipped fingers and toes lay just ahead, like a crouching beast ready to pounce. A season of joy became a time of unease and worry. Would we receive our ration of coal? Would it be sent to the military preparing for war in Europe? Or would it be seized by "speculators" and sold elsewhere for a better price? That is what we would hear, rumors forming like icicles from eaves in winter.

Even as I sat there, the coal furnace below us rumbled to life like a monster wakening. Yet punishing memories of cold continued to flare bright as the morning sun. I had control over heat now, but I did not then. Sometimes, it seemed no one did.

It is difficult to compare The Howard then with Brooklyn now. I am a child no longer, but I was at that time. Different eyes, a different way of seeing the world. But the memories insist, and the comparison follows.

There was much about The Howard Orphanage at Indian Head, much about Kings Park, I liked. But there is really no easy comparison to Brooklyn. I love my life here, love the city. As has been said by others well before me, it is where my heart lies.

I have heard someone refer to the country as "maternal," the city as "paternal." *She* and *he*. More likely, I read it. Whoever it was described the country as wider, softer, quieter, its branching arms reaching to embrace. The city, in turn, was narrower, harder, louder, a place of cocked elbows used to create space. "Colder" was also a word used to describe the city. Whoever thought that never spent a winter on Long Island. Flat as it was, there was nothing to intercept abiding wind with its icy teeth.

But when people describe New York City, they say "the city." In other words, "it." The same was true for Kings Park or The Howard Orphanage. I have done it, still do.

When I allow myself to think about it, "city" and "country," it is not so simple for me. Put it in mother / father terms, each place possesses something of both. For me, they are just different. Again, as an adult, I have eyes to behold the city. When it comes to The Howard, I have only a child's memories. Some of those memories have tattered and faded like an old flag left out too long. Then too, country living was not a choice. For me, it was exile from those I loved most.

I see the city as a marriage between the maternal and the paternal, if you will. The city *is* harder in some ways, so little space for so many people. And it *is* louder, people weaving on the streets, churning to get somewhere. I do believe country people move more slowly, and I am not sure why. Perhaps part of it is because they do not have to jostle for room.

In some ways, it might be easier to see the

country as a better place to live. Even with woods everywhere, it left me with a wide-open feeling, its ample space containing few people. You are freer to let your mind wander, to let it drift like dandelion fluff.

In the city, you cannot do that. You must be alert on the street, watching where you walk, knowing where you are going. If not, you could be run over by an automobile or, even worse, one of those new motorized trucks. There are still many horses pulling heavy carts that could crush you if you fell under one. Then, there are trolleys to dodge, and power-lines that sometimes come down. At train stations, you must remain on your toes at all times. And all of this is going on simultaneously, a beehive of swarming activity. Look left, look right, left again, front, back, front once more. Only then, do you dare cross a street.

Streets? Streets are like a mismatched quilt. Here and there are stretches of the smooth, new blacktop, often grooved by trolley tracks. If you are not careful, you can trip or catch a heel. A block away, you might find anything from tarred macadam to cobblestones. In more distant sections of Brooklyn, the streets remain unpaved. After a good rain, a team of horses might be needed to pull an automobile from the muck.

Buildings in the country are generally simpler, and again, spread out. In the city, they are bunched tightly like soldiers with motley uniforms. Rows of stately brownstones are often disrupted by a jumble of dwellings, most rising three or four stories. When you gaze at the city, you look up. In the country, your eyes travel outward.

No matter the differences, I love the city. It is my home, the place where the people I love dwell. It may seem at times a cold, drably-dressed lady, but I feel her warmth. (So much for "paternal.")

When I look up, I see lofty church spires, noble in their reach. From the height of an elevated train station, you can see many of them, their spires pointing to Heaven. At The Howard in Kings Park, chapel services were held in a cottage.

I know it is an unfair comparison, that church is a state of mind. But in the city, churches draw you with their steepled towers, stained glass, and in some cases, immensity. Inside, dark wood, the smell of rose water, and the siren choir call pull you to your knees. You become quiet – body, mind, soul. You do not just stop talking or begin whispering; your spirit calms. And all this before the sermon even begins.

Most churches are open-doored and welcoming. You can enter at any time, not just on Sunday. A church is like a safe place for the surrounding neighborhood, a refuge for lost souls. A place to remember why you do what you do the rest of the week should weariness lead you to forget.

During the cold season, when you look up, you see plumes of smoke curling skyward from soot-blackened chimneys. If I close my eyes while I sip tea, I feel as if I am in Olde England. Why "olde" with an "e?" I think it has to do with mystery. Enchantment. It is as if for a magical moment I have traveled back in time. I slowly fill with energy, ready to stride toward the day.

In the city, you have to find what you need,

but it is there in abundance. You do not have to travel far to find it. Frequently it comes to you on a horse-drawn cart. At The Howard, provisions were delivered to us. Everything we were going to have was there, if not abundant.

I believe fear of fire is greater in the city, if for no other reason than the clustered houses. Though electric lights have sprouted everywhere, oil lamps and candles are still widely used. At night, you see them flickering like dancing fairies. But accidentally knock one over or forget to put it out at bedtime? Look out! It is the same with kerosene heaters. People resort to the older ways when they lack money for the light bill or a load of coal.

Some might argue this point, but for me, there are more unpleasant smells in the city. I once heard a man selling pumpkins claim "horse apples smell the same city or country, one."

True, but at The Howard, the air did smell cleaner. And when they mowed hay or harvested the fruit trees, it was even better. In Brooklyn, the smell from a bakery can leave me hesitant to move beyond its reassuring aroma. The same is true for the air above a chunk of ice. But within a block, scorched metal, burning rubber, or ozone from trolley wires can overwhelm anything pleasant.

The same might be said for colors. Thanks to Nature – flowers, sky, woods – colors in the country are lavish. Yet, within the somber tones of the city, you notice color more, receive it like a sacrament. Sunlight through stained glass, storefront window dressings, a pot of pink and purple geraniums against rusted grillwork. I notice the splashes of color even more when it rains, probably a reason why I love rain.

My shivering just stopped, the house is warm, and so am I. I hear the children stirring. They will chat in bed for a bit, but they will soon be in here with me. Catherine hugging my neck, Dorothy climbing in my lap, they will be clamoring for hot oatmeal. And it will be ready for them, as am I. My day begins.

Chapter Twenty-One: The Great Circle of Life Turns

Growing up, my hopes included life with children. Now I can no longer imagine one without them. They are my life, shaping almost everything I do.

I believe there is a will in all people to create a work that will outlive us. I suspect that desire ties in with the knowledge that we will not last. Something original wells up in us, and as we shape it, it shapes us. But of all the things we create, what could be more important than a child? The future depends on how well we complete the task. It takes longer to create a finished person than most great works of art. I also believe a loving parent best fills the artist's role from birthing an idea to buffing the masterpiece.

It is not that there was a want of love at The Howard. There were caring people – housemothers, teachers, workmen, administrators. But what they could give had to be shared by 250 children. They could only give it in the cracks between their own daily chores. The hands-on of a parent who helped you become *you* in a way you could cherish was missing. Well, not totally absent, but it was inconstant, and in that, not enough. There was no substitute for a parent, someone who belonged to you and to whom you belonged.

I have spoken to my husband about my years

at the orphanage, of my memories as an "inmate." I have tried to describe the experience to him as best I know how. You live off-balance, unsure of who you are, knowing where you belong, but not how to get there. If something happens to one of us, the other will do whatever it takes to keep the family together.

The glue that holds all of the pieces of a creation together is love. Without it, like food each day, you live with a part of you hollowed out, uneasy with hunger. Separated from those you love, everything becomes *maybe*. It is hard to trust that whatever seems real today, will be there tomorrow.

My children need to grow up believing in what they can touch, safe in their feelings. They need to be at ease with the love we have for them. They need to believe it is there forever, can never be withdrawn, nor will it be.

Our days, even Sunday to an extent, are work-filled – John at the Post Office, I at home. But with hard work and fatigue, comes much joy, especially with cooling days and cooler autumn nights. The evenings delightful, once the children are in bed, we can sit on the front stoop and chat.

I love this time of year. I can release my thoughts once again, my mind at peace. Amidst summer's dog days, parched from the heat, it is difficult to find a cool mind. At night, minds toasted after a day's labor, it is not uncommon to hear raised voices paint-peeling. People shouting, dogs barking, trolley wheels screeching, the sounds are almost as trying as the unforgiving heat.

The days are bearable now. In August, we would sit out front after dark, sip something cold and just breathe. We would breathe as if we had just run a race, too tired to say much of anything. Now, graced by a cool breeze, we can speak of our children and why we strive for them.

Aside from the mercy of coolness, even blindfolded, you would know it is autumn from the smells, from the way they gentle the senses. Gone are the vendors selling iced lemonade. Carts roll by now selling roasted nuts, hot potatoes and pretzels. Sometimes, it is the aroma that announces them.

I believe the sense of smell is somehow keener in autumn. Maybe the cool releases it or maybe I just imagine it. But I smell flowers better, the asters and the chrysanthemums. It is not exactly a perfumed scent, but one of the Earth. I smell it in fresh vegetables as if the tillage they grew in still clings to them. I smell meat cooking, baked bread unwrapped and set out, Ivory-soaped children.

Recently, a knife grinder came by and sharpened two of my carving knives. When he was not pedaling his grinding stone, with his permission, I touched it. It was the roughest surface I have ever touched, harder than a landlord's heart. Much rougher than an emery board for filing nails.

While he worked a knife against the wheel, it was like an assault on all the senses. Orange sparks flew into the twilight like electric embers, the screech of metal on stone almost painful. No wonder the man is almost deaf. You have to repeat everything you say to him two, sometimes three times. You might want to laugh, but I could feel metal grit in my teeth, could taste it. My ears rang for hours.

When he finished and left the neighborhood,

I felt the balm of quiet. There is beauty in stillness, a soul calm we are losing with motor cars on top of trolleys.

I found myself watching pigeons landing nearby, pacing, begging for breadcrumbs. A few of our neighbors built coops on the flat rooftops, and run flocks from them. The two-beat movements of these birds and their cooing relax me.

In a way, the pigeons have become our pets. Pets, otherwise, are a luxury few working people can afford.

Pigeon-watching eventually led me back to thoughts of my children, my flock. Pets may be a luxury, but children are a necessity. With them, the great circle of life turns.

"You cold?" John said to me.

"A little," I said.

"Like me to fetch your shawl?"

"Uh-uh," I said, placing his arm around my shoulders. He squeezed.

"Think I'll head upstairs, check on the kids," he said, facing me, his breath minty.

"Not yet," I said, clutching his arm tighter. My voice was mostly matter-of-fact with just a touch of a plea.

Even in the rapidly advancing dusk, I could see him smile.

My husband's arm around my shoulders, better than any shawl, I think of Dukie, a truly dutiful boy. He lives with his grandparents, the Reverend and Mrs. Hamlin. Because of it, I see him in a different way from my other children – at a distance. I do not get to see him as often, but I like what I see.

I am not sure he will be tall, none of us are, but I believe he will be sturdy. He is already broad-shouldered, solid in construction. I believe he will become a steadfast man, resolute in character, ready to do what needs doing. Perhaps I love him more, if that is possible, for the separation. I do not know what I would do without him.

I believe Catherine, my second child and oldest daughter, has an ounce of deviltry in her. You can catch it glimmer in her mischievous eyes, in the way she carries herself. The pride in the lift of her head speaks to a spiritedness unmatched by her siblings. She is not as careful with words as Dorothy, but she is also a good child. A wild hair just missed brushing against her, but her spunk promises a strong, determined character. She may have her way, but she will do it with humor and sparkle.

Dorothy is my quiet child (most of the time). I wonder if some of it has to do with the wandering eye leaving her self-conscious. I try not to dwell on it, but her head was damaged at delivery, left misshapened by an inept intern. For months, my mother, Kate, remolded the baby's head and eye position. To a skeptic, I would say, "You didn't see it; I did." In any event, it bonded them, pod to pea, Dorothy "Nana's baby" whenever they meet. Dorothy is a loving child with a sweet little laugh, soft-spoken like me. Not yet six, she already loves to look at books. I believe she will acquire language like a bee gathers pollen. It will just stick to her as her curiosity takes her from book to book.

Dorothy, in particular, likes to help me, for example polishing silver. I must admit to a twinge of guilt, I do not mind letting her do it. She also helps with her younger sisters, Irene and Thelma. Dorothy and Thelma, my baby, are like entwining vines with each other. Dorothy loves to mother her, and Thelma is a sponge for it. It helps me so much when I cannot locate a third hand for what has to be done.

Irene and Thelma are little more than toddlers, their personalities beginning to burst forth like spring buds. But, as with all my children, they seem happy, and for that, I am thankful. If they were not, I am not sure how I could manage, with one more on the way.

I feel tired lately, more than usual. It leaves me wondering how I will find the space and energy, for one more child. But I truly believe if I find room in my heart, we will find room in our world. And I will.

Chapter Twenty-Two: The Spear Point

We were looking for arrowheads around Hog Pond.

It was a Sunday afternoon in May at The Howard when I found one. Or rather, when it found me. In bare feet (we usually were from late spring through early autumn) I stepped on something sharp.

Hopping on the other foot, I gazed at the spot, my hand clamped over my mouth. I found what I thought was a stone. Bending to rub my throbbing foot, I saw that the stone was an almost perfect point.

I tried to pick it up, but the stone was wedged in the hard-packed, sandy soil. I then picked around it, scooping the wet sand away with my fingers. A pinkish-white point emerged, so beautifully perfect in its hammered shape, I barely noticed its imperfections. I began to wiggle it until the Earth, as if unwilling, released it with a gravelly hiss. It was the largest arrowhead I had ever seen. It even had a curved tail like a fish. In fact, turn it sideways, it looked like a fish.

"I found one! I found one!" I hollered to the others with me. "I found an arrowhead!"

The others immediately crowded around. This was a big deal, the "Real McCoy" as they say, a genuine arrowhead, not just a flake. I was holding something maybe a thousand years old. Reverend Gordon, the superintendent, later told me it could have been older, much older. He died in 1914, a year or two before I left. Some said it was from working too much. I believe it. He never stopped trying to help us, working his fingers and toes to the bone. After his death, his wife, the "matron" took over.

Hog Pond was special, a rarity I was told, on Long Island, a freshwater source above ground. With its sandy soil, Long Island rainfall generally vanished into the earth. Maybe it was fed by an underground well, but no one seemed to know.

Because of the scattered pieces of human activity, it was rumored that Indians had camped there for centuries. I believed it was true. There was too much there for only a rumor.

In the winter, the pond would freeze, and we could walk or slide on it. And fall. Some of the inmates would pretend they were skaters gliding across the ice, their arms folded behind them. Except they could not glide; the ice was too rough and uneven. A few of the older boys would try to smooth it with a shovel. All that work to pretend. No one had skates you could use. The skates donated were so old the ankle supports had worn out.

In warm weather, the pond was a great place for finding bits and pieces of the past. But just that – in pieces. Rarely did we find anything as it had been made. The arrowheads were usually so small, you could not be sure it was an arrowhead or a flake. But this arrowhead, was so large, it was hard to believe it could have been any bigger. How would a shaft have held it?

According to one of the teachers the next day, an arrow shaft could not have held it. It was too large, too heavy.

139

"I believe that is a spear point," she said.

For a day or so, I was the Cat's Meow. Or, at least my spear-point was. It became the centerpiece for the following week's history, geography and science lessons. Questions whanged off the walls. How old was it? Who made it? How did they make it? Stones to shape stones? What was it made of? Teacher said she thought it was quartz, but could not be sure.

It was fun being special, almost like being famous. Somebody who discovered something important. But it did not last very long. The spear-point ended up on a shelf in the classroom, forgotten by others. Invisible spiders cobwebbed it. When light touched the silk, it looked as if the spear-point had been tied down. It brought to mind *Gulliver's Travels*.

Seeing it that way left me wistful. I had not forgotten it. My thoughts turned to the past, not so much sad as reflective. Well, maybe a little bit lonesome. Maybe more than a little bit.

I would think of my parents in Brooklyn. I could not help it. Any time loneliness managed to squeeze through the door to my life, my thoughts would turn to family.

It had not been so hard when The Howard was still in Brooklyn. I was never lonely in the Crown Heights section, what we called Weeksville. My parents lived in the same neighborhood. Most days, I could catch a glimpse of them and wave. I would wave whether they saw me or not. John Henry and I got to see them almost every weekend.

When The Howard moved to Kings Park,

loneliness slipped in and pitched an invisible tent. It was always lurking, ready to pounce on someone feeling sorry for herself. I tried hard not to let that happen, but sometimes....

Anyway, the spear-point on the shelf. Someone told us Indians traveling to Long Island Sound and the Nissequogue River camped at the pond. They came "to fish and shell." Maybe they were looking for those tiny shells from which they made wampum. I cannot think of the name, but I believe it started with a "C." Someone else said, "No, they lived here. Where else were they going to find fresh water?"

I thought, "Why not both?" Since they wandered from place to place depending on the season, they probably lived in several places. Maybe *home* was where they were at that moment in their travels. That thought helped me push loneliness back out the door. Or at least into a closet.

Cowrie. That is the word, I believe, for the shells. *Cowrie*.

I found myself stirred by thoughts of Indians living here, right where we stood. A few thousand years ago they were hunting, fishing, berrying, making tools. Did they smile as they worked, maybe laugh a bit? Or hum as I do? Did someone let her voice rise in song, maybe lift her face to the sun? Find those tiny joys that are always there amidst the unending toil? Did they offer them to the children in quick breaks from the work?

More likely, the women invented a game they played with their children while they continued working. It is what I do today.

But back then at The Howard, I wondered what Indians had to endure. Separation from family? Probably not. Families traveled together. Some might view a wandering life as primitive. It probably was hard, but families were together.

Was loneliness a problem, camping out with them? I doubt it. *Loneliness* was probably lonely. Families lived with other families that depended on each other, what we call a community, like Weeksville.

What about orphans? Their bands were small, and could be reduced in so many ways. With only early medicine to turn to, a simple infection from a cut could prove fatal. But they did not have to worry about money, only to survive. And the means to do it lay about them. It explained at least some of their travels. I imagine an orphan would have been taken in by another family within the band. The survival of the group depended on it.

I wondered what happened when one band or tribe met another. Warfare? Possibly. But with small numbers, if survival was foremost in importance, they probably tried to avoid each other. That or get along. I suspect weapons were primarily for the hunt, for finding food, for survival.

Within this freedom allowed by territory of their own, I also wondered if these Indians kept slaves. Some Indian tribes did. I read it, forget where. But unlike our slavery, it was done to replenish lost tribesmen and women. Indian slaves could be adopted into the tribe, gaining full and equal membership. Again, it strikes me that the number one purpose of a tribe was survival. I keep coming back to that.

My eyes would now and then return to the spear-point. I would wonder, what did it kill? A deer? Maybe even a bear? It was too large for small animals.

On occasion, my wonderings about the point would set off thoughts about age and truth. Some grown-ups claimed the Earth is no more than a few thousand years old. Yet according to Reverend Gordon, the spear-point could have been that old. Did the Earth come with spear-points and arrowheads? Did someone not have to make them?

I wanted to ask the question, but I did not. I was afraid I might upset an adult if he could not come up with an answer.

But there it was, webbed to the shelf, a beautiful pinkish-white point, chipped to its perfect shape. Buried for so many years, wedged in weather-beaten sand and gravel, it pushed up. Or the Earth pushed it up. One day nothing, the next, there I am stepping on it. It was like finding buried treasure or a lost work of art.

I truly believe the Earth will yield its secrets if you look for them. But it will also hold back a few for the sake of mystery. Which brings me to the latest mystery growing in me, now more than four months. Come March, another secret will push out into the world and be revealed.

Chapter Twenty-Three: Recess

In 1917, the Brooklyn Ice Palace opened. Corner of Bedford and Atlantic, it is the largest ice-skating rink in New York City. People who loved to skate now could do it all year round.

I believe Catherine, my live wire, would live there if she could. Adventuresome as she is, I am not surprised she was drawn to it. Almost seven, she is already learning to skate, and I believe she has a flair for it. Whenever there is an opportunity to go to the Palace, all I hear is "Mama, Mama! Please, please, *please*! Pretty please with a cherry on top."

I believe she could give a beggar a few pointers. And if each "please" was a penny falling from Heaven, we would be rich. I dread when she will want the more expensive figure skates. We will put that day off as long as possible.

I remember when a few of us at The Howard were given skates to share. They were hand-me-downs, the leather so worn the ankle support was gone. I remain grateful for what we had, but like much of what was donated, the skates were useless. At Hog Pond in winter, we would watch a few "Townies" from Kings Park. They had good skates, and would glide along while we shuffled about, shuffled and fell mostly.

A few of the Townies laughed at us. One of our older boys overheard a Townie say, "Those colored kids can't skate, no how." Never mind the condition of our skates, another offered an explanation. "That's 'cause there's no ice in Africa." If the time comes, when it comes, we will somehow get Catherine the skates she needs.

For now, the Ice Palace – the world of ice – is Catherine's dreamland. When she cannot skate, she wants to watch other skaters glide by, studying the way they move. I believe she is committing their routines and tricks to memory, preparing for her time. Often, she appears entranced by the organ music and the sound of skates hissing on the icy surface.

The Ice Palace will sell "ice time" to non-skaters who shuffle along in shoes. They must stay close to the rail, away from the whirlpool of skaters. The inner portion of the oval belongs to the really good skaters practicing their spinning, leaping movements.

There is something about ice that acts like a magnet. (I was going to say it can *freeze* you, but what a terrible joke.) In summer, it provides relief from days of unmerciful heat. You hear "Ice Man!" and without thinking, you find yourself hurrying as a child to a treat. He is like the Pied Piper, and we are, all of us, the children of Hamelin. Only the iceman does not need a pipe. His ice is the siren song.

But it is more than that. Wrapped in burlap, vapors pour from the blocks of ice on his cart, flowing downward. I cannot imagine inhaling opium could be better than a whiff of ice on a roasting day.

It is also the *cool* of it. So obvious, it sounds silly, does it not? I do not mean simply that ice is cold. "Cold" is when it enters your mouth. But "cool" is how it touches you without you touching it. Close enough, you feel it like a breeze against your face, running over your skin and hands. At such a time, it is difficult to think dark thoughts.

Think of something unpleasant – the smell of sparks from a trolley-line or worse, the sparks singeing your skin. For me, it would be the smell of mothballs or the chafing of wet wool. Then try to imagine your nose inches from an ice block. Ah-h!

The pleasure of ice got me thinking about other pleasures, "diversions" as they say in the newspapers. I think of it all as "recess." I know, it probably sounds like my mind is back in PS 28. "Recess" was the time outside of classwork when we ran, jumped, or just *were* for a little while. It was like catching your breath after a race. I still think of a break from chores – *any* break – as recess.

When we were children, anything could be recess, a way to shift your mind to something fun. The junkman going by, his horse dropping "green apples" as often as something fell off his cart. It seemed for every two scraps he threw on the pile, one fell off. He wanted metal, but would take just about anything.

Back then, very little was thrown out. Food? Everything was eaten. Bones went into soup or fed a dog. There were always scruffy-thin alley dogs around, trying to survive. Peelings, rinds and pits were fed to gardens. Even the horse apples – there was always someone shoveling them up to fertilize a tomato patch. Clothes? They were handed down, given away or worn until they tattered beyond repair. Before I would let that happen, I would cut them up and sew them into curtains or armchair coverings. If nothing else, I would use them for cleaning rags. I suspect junkmen probably came along when we began to throw things out.

Recess. I was getting a bit high and mighty there, just full of myself. Back to recess. Give a child a spoon, a marble, a worn-out belt, and she will figure out something to do with it. She will start digging with it or rolling or whip-snapping it. Give it to two children? If they do not squabble over it, they will invent a game.

Allow the children a street, sidewalk, wall or board fence, they will use it for a game. Chalk a few squares of the sidewalk, it becomes a court for hopscotch or jump rope. The street turns into a racing track or a ball field. How many games have been created bouncing an old castaway handball against a wall or wooden fence?

Adults? We have our diversions. Beyond Sunday services, church is central to our lives with its social activities, music, singing and dancing. There is nothing I enjoy more than sitting on our apartment steps in the evening, conversing with John. Maybe add another couple or two, but no more. More? I tend to quiet down. I like the intimacy, the chance to know how someone else thinks. I also like for them to know what I think, if they are willing to listen. It gives me the chance to see how what I say lands on the ears of others.

Sometimes, we will break into song. Someone will start popping his fingers, and we hitch a melody to the beat. "Stagger Lee" is perfect for *a capella*. So is the "St. Louis Blues" or "Ballin' the

Jack." Before long, people are leaning from windows, standing in doorways, listening, tapping their toes. My heart taps along with them. For me, this is pure happiness. I do not need to paint the town red to find it.

On July 4th, we might go to Prospect Park to picnic and listen to the band concert. I love to sing along with the patriotic airs: "Yankee Doodle Dandy" or "Pack up Your Troubles." "America the Beautiful." "My Country 'tis of Thee." I know, but I love music. When I sing, I feel I am part of something, a part of everything.

Once or twice each summer, we travel – walk, take the El, walk some more – to Coney Island. I love to sit on the sand and feel the sun's embrace. I cannot close my eyes (the children and water) but I imagine I am rocking in a lullaby.

And wonder of wonders, we now have moving pictures. They say "speakies" are about to follow. Oh my!

Recently, John and I saw *Ben-Hur*. It was quite a spectacle. I almost disappeared into the story until I realized white actors were playing brown and black-skinned people. I have seen pictures of Asia Minor in *National Geographic Magazine* (I believe it was in a doctor's waiting room), and the people were not white. They were people of color.

I do not know what this has to do with recess. I just happened to remember it when I saw *Ben-Hur*. I could say, "I wonder why they used white actors for people of color." But I do not. I think I already know.

With adults, it is not that simple, and I am not sure why. But adult diversions noted, we do not seem to play as much even when we can. Some might say it is because of time and energy – no time, no energy. To an extent that is true, but that does not explain it, at least not for me.

It seems to me that sometimes, adults have to turn to children to remember how to play. When we do not, when we fail to remember how, that is when we can become troubled. Even worse, that is when we can get into trouble. An adult, who has forgotten recess, may turn to an illegal diversion – gambling, racing, smoking opium, drinking alcohol. Other things.

When we join in the game, we accomplish two things. We quickly recall the joy of play, and we make our children happy by doing so. They see us as they often do not, in a way that shows we still feel joy. My children love it when I play with them.

When I can, I take them to one of the parks or playgrounds within walking distance. To do it, I have to plan as if we are going on a trip. I try to work it when possible around one of Dukie's visits. Either I pick him up at my in-laws, or they bring him over for the day. Almost everyone has to carry something – Dukie, Catherine, Dorothy. Even Irene, little as she is. I carry Thelma. At the same time, we stay close, not wandering until we get to the park. When we cross a street, we do it as one, hands held tight, *no* letting go.

Fulton Park and Brower Park are the two easiest to reach on foot without wearing the children out. Brower, in particular, is one of my favorites. It is a small, lovely park, great for ease of mind – an Eden in the city. You feel as if you stepped through an invisible curtain into a wonderland of trees and flowers. The kids love it because Brooklyn Children's Museum is there, and they let children touch things. St. John's Park is not far, but it is more for older children and adults involved with athletics.

We once walked to Lincoln Terrace Park, but afterward, I decided it was too far. Strangely, you could see an anti-aircraft gun there from The Great War. The "war to end all wars" some have said. Wishful thinking to my mind, I would still love to believe it. The gun was supposedly hidden, but it was not. Were they expecting we would be attacked? The thought was chilling watching my children play. Was this what happened in Europe? At that point, I could bear to think of it no longer.

For my children, I believe the New Lots Playground at the eastern end of Weeksville is their favorite. It is not far from our church. Built in 1920, it is a place for everyone, but Heaven for children. With its monkey bars, swings, see-saws and slides, I get to watch the children squealing with joy.

And yet, elbowing into my mind like a dark presence, is the thought of what lies ahead for them. I cannot help but wonder, will they be up to it? Can I prepare them for the world to come, a world that may not treasure them? I do not permit this line of thought to go on at length. Sad as I might be for a moment, I will not allow bitterness to tag along.

Instead, I will refocus my mind. I will think about the years at The Howard, singing with The Quartette. We once sang at the Masonic Kismet Shrine in Brooklyn, a fundraiser, of course. I remember standing at the Nostrand Avenue elevated station, looking at the onion domes of the Shrine. It was like looking into another world, oriental, exotic, mysterious. When I want to clear my mind, I picture the domes and wonder, how did they build them?

If that does not work, I will switch to something more immediate, something that speaks through the senses. The smell of hot cocoa or coffee in winter. The taste of vanilla ice cream in summer. A cool breeze sliding down a warm afternoon to caress my face. And *ice*.

I visualize the colors of ice. That is right, colors, not just white by day or black at night. And not just with the lights of The Ice Palace, shivering across its icy surface. Watch a patch of ice in daylight or, even better, an icicle. Walk around it. Moving from shadow to sun, it shimmers like a chameleon, silver to blue-green to a radiant blue. Each color stunning in its own right. Ice, offering a window into life.

Chapter Twenty-Four: More Strange Math

I spoke of some of the "strange math" I have seen in my life.

I notice when figures do not figure, now more than ever. I believe that comes from trying to stretch a dollar every day. If you are trying to find the two dollars you need for the one you have, you know. But this is not about how hard John and I work for that one dollar. This is not a sob story. This is a break-your-heart story. And it begins with the strangest, blood-chilling math yet.

How did $250 - 1 = 0$?

It began with the failure to deliver The Howard's coal shipment in the unforgiving winter of $1917 - 1918$. Extreme cold and mounting neglect led to the death of The Howard Orphanage and Industrial School.

John Henry and I had returned to Brooklyn in 1915, but to our sorrow, we heard about it. Weaned on my mother's rule-heavy religion, I flooded with a choking guilt I was unable to voice.

I have heard many rumors of what happened, many explanations. But I do not believe an explanation is an excuse, ever.

Supposedly, the war effort (The Great War. The war to end all wars. Really?) "requisitioned" our coal. *Requisitioned.* A polite word for "took." That would mean our military took for its men the heating coal destined for children – *colored* children. The world being what it is, I still do not want to believe it.

Another rumor, one I would prefer to believe, is that the coal was sold by shameless profiteers. "Speculators." Sounds like a fancy word for "crooks." I prefer to believe this evil was the "work" of individuals wanting consciences than the willful act of a government. Either way, the end result was tragedy.

By January of 1918, in the midst of a bitterly cold winter, 250 colored children were slowly freezing. Despite the efforts of the acting superintendent and the Directors, the orphanage was unable to find another source. A diet of sleet, snow and wind – Long Island wind, the kind with fangs – kept temperatures below freezing. The suffering continued for weeks. Most of the staff stood by the children and battled to find help. But it was rumored that a few abandoned them. That was so painful to think about, I refused to believe it. I left it as a rumor, and no more.

In the end, as I understood it, people from Kings Park rescued the children. I have no details as to how this came about, only that it happened. The children were picked up in various stages of damage from the cold, and secured in private homes. Several of them were suffering from frostbite, two so severe their feet were amputated.

Eventually, after proper medical treatment, the children were "dispersed" to other orphanages in the New York area. The Howard Orphanage was no longer, its fifty-year existence gone. Vanished. And once again, because of a lack of funds. The shoestring it always depended on had snapped.

A few voices were raised in criticism of the staff at The Howard. Why did "they" not do something sooner? How could "they" let this happen? It seems always a *"they"* critics turn to when they themselves cannot find someone to blame. Well, the staff was colored, bred on Mr. Booker T. Washington's philosophy of self-sufficiency. Maybe they kept trying to do it themselves rather than appear lacking in the eyes of the white world. They had managed to keep the orphanage alive for 50 years on a trickle of fickle charity. Then, when nature dealt a death blow, it was *their* fault? That might soothe the wobbly conscience of a distant critic who could have helped, but chose not to. If blame deserved to be placed, it belonged to a nation that chooses uncertain charity over public programs.

Attempts were made to reorganize the orphanage in Brooklyn, to no avail. Again, the funds could not be found. No philanthropists stepped forward to help this time. Surprise? No. Colored children fell toward the bottom of the list of public and private concerns. At the bottom, that is, if they were even on it. This might sound bitter, but I prefer to see it as a fact. As I have said before, sad, *YES*, but bitter? Hopefully not.

Another fact, by the spring of 1918, all the assets of The Howard had been sold – animals, buildings, land. *That* tested my faith! Almost overnight, the property of The Howard had been auctioned. It may sound harsh, but I felt as if it had been plundered. All those people to grab up a piece of it, but none to keep it going.

It felt as if a house had been torn down around the people living in it. I know that may sound dramatic, but that is what powerful feelings often do. They affect us dramatically. At least, they do me.

And what of the children who knew only The Howard in their lives? *Dispersed*? Dispersed to what? Another institution? A private home funded by the state? To begin with so little, then to have to begin again, adjusting to a new world. Were dear friends separated? Probably. Brothers and sisters?

All those children had already been "dispersed" by life only to be dispersed once more. How could they ever believe in anything stable, that anything could endure? How could they ever trust? Someone had given birth to them. Did they let themselves wonder where that person was? Who she was? Did she still exist? Was there anyone to find even if they looked? I am judging neither the women nor the men. I was not there. I do not know the circumstances. Look at mine. But a part of me goes with them wherever they may go.

I cry when I think about it for more than a few moments. I become ill imagining if John Henry and I had been separated.

Separation. It becomes a fact the moment the seed of life takes. Choose to, you could imagine life as a series of separations – birth, leaving home, losing a beloved, death. Those are among the normal separations, the ones you are expected to stand up to. You adjust to them, and move to the next stage.

There are others we do not expect – loss of a parent as a child, abandonment, broken trust. Those and others test us beyond the "normal" separations.

They can separate us from the belief that what we do plays any part in what happens. They can leave us marooned on an island in our minds from which there is no escape. If there is no escape, what does it matter what we do? And who cares for the separated?

The first major separation is childbirth. Expecting my sixth, it is probably not surprising where my thoughts are settling. Childbirth is something women understand, and I believe, men cannot. They can observe it, try to imagine it, and sit in sympathy. What can one say for those who remain apart in detachment or horror? But none of them can *know*. I am not sure what else I could add to that.

My husband has asked me more than once, "How do you do it?"

I hear it as praise, and smile, but I really do not know how to answer him. My body does it, aided by the will of God. I am on a journey I have no control over, nor can I be certain of the destination. I cannot shorten or lengthen it, depending on how I am feeling. Neither can I will away the nausea nor order a baby of a certain disposition from a Sears catalogue. With all that Macy's sells, I cannot go there and specify the child I want. As if I could. Or would.

So how do I do what I do about a pregnancy until birth? Since what I try to do is accept what happens, I am not sure that is the question. For nine months, I undergo body and mind-tugging changes that can leave me a stranger to myself. Maybe forever. A better question might be how do I manage to hold onto an image of who I am? That is a part I do have some control over.

On occasion, a man will describe childbirth as "woman's work." Detached, he sees it as something he has little or no part in. Rather than doing it together, he leaves it to his wife and shows up consciously at the birth. That will ruffle my feathers for some of us die from it.

I think about the dangerous work some men do, work that could cost them their lives. Firefighting, police work, iron workers on skyscrapers – so true. But more women die every year doing "women's work" than men do in any job. If an army lost as many men, I believe there would be an uproar demanding an explanation. When it is "woman's work"? Silence.

Am I hearing a strain of bitterness here? I hope not. At the moment, I do not even feel angry. It is just my way of recognizing a reality that men who shape the world often skip over.

All of that said, my life is full. They tell us that the world is now at peace. Though I wonder about that, I hope it is true. The failure of The League of Nations has left me uncertain.

It is now mid-October in Brooklyn. I am at peace sitting on my stoop, lulled once more by those cool autumn breezes. The leaves on the trees have turned, and most of them have fallen. Asters and chrysanthemums have replaced the flowers of summer.

Leafless trees bring out the artists of the city, painting and photographing the branches against the sky. It brings to mind lace on a sleeve. If I shut my eyes and hear music, I feel as if I am in Paris.

People around us seem to be making it

financially, as we are – barely. When that burden eases even the tiniest of bits, life becomes so much more bearable. I am able to enjoy it as I believe it was meant to be. I have the family I have always wanted with one more on the way.

Yet, grateful as I am, each pregnancy, each birth, takes so much out of me, I do not seem to come back quite as far. If I were running a race, the starting line would be farther away, the finish more grueling. For nine months, I grow larger, appear flush with life. But that baby needs everything I have, everything I can bring to it. If it nurtures well, do I then nurture less well? Do I drain of the things I need to flourish? For certain, the birthing itself is draining as nothing else is. When you are finished, you have nothing left to give. The reward – the love your child evokes. While I consider this a fair trade in my mind, I am no longer certain my body agrees.

I have discussed this with a few other women, my mother and mother-in-law included. One or two have been discomforted by my question and took shelter in "the Lord will provide." Okay. But almost all of them have experienced the condition as I have. Their reality is also mine. To know that helped. I had begun to question myself, wondering if I was ungrateful for the bounty bestowed upon me. The word "tired" came up a lot in our conversations.

John and I have discussed making this the last addition to our family, if we can, God willing. Oh-oh, I hear Thelma! She just woke from her nap and is letting me know she wants me lickety split.

Chapter Twenty-Five: Yesterday, a Part of Today

When I write about something in the past, I find myself slipping into the present. I have noticed I tend to do that even when I try not to. Though I wonder about it, I think I know why it happens. For me, what is past, no matter how long ago, is only a thought, smell or blink away.

Some say, "The past is past." Is it? I think people who say that, do not want to think about it. For me, it is so real, as real as if it is happening right now. I remember something, and my muscles twitch as if they owned that memory. My stomach stirs, odors rise up and set off more memories. And voices? I do not remember voices so much as I hear them. It is like a waking dream. For me, yesterday will always be part of today. Probably part of tomorrow, too.

Someone took a photograph of The Howard from a hill, a wide view that captured Indian Head Farm. The photograph was taken in winter, the trees leafless skeletons, the ground cake-frosted with snow.

Something strange happened when I squinted, attempting to look at it through one eye. Part of the picture disappeared. I then used my hand to cover one half of the picture while I viewed the other. It was eerie. The right side of the picture, filled with our magnificent barns and animals, appeared like a New England postcard. You could even see a person or two. It was so lovely, it looked drawn rather than real.

The left side suggested a different world, stark and so cold, just looking at it left you shivering. The farther to the left the eye traveled, the bleaker it became. To the far left sat our cottages in an empty, wind-swept field away from everything.

Look at the right side, I would think of words like "secure," "pastoral," "inviting." The left, I thought of "adrift," "isolated," "apart." Same place, same scene, same moment, but two different worlds. To the right, even the word "warmth" might jump out at you as you viewed the scene. Left, ultimately to the undoing of The Howard, children in those cottages were struggling to stay warm.

The photograph set off a meteor shower of memories, most of them autumn leading into winter. The smell of fresh milk from the dairy, a skim of cream still there even after separation. Blue sky over the gloomy gray water of Long Island Sound. Animals bleating by day; at night, the creak of the cooling cottage and the hoot of an owl.

Someone once told me of an old Indian tale that the call of an owl announced a coming death. Probably the one who heard it. I respect traditions, but the more I thought about it, it made no sense. Someone is always dying, but so is someone always entering the light. The call soothed me, left me feeling safe as I fell asleep, the owl watching over us.

In autumn, the air filled with wood smoke and leaf fires, with decay and mold, dirt after rain. Somehow, it always seemed cleaner, as if something was beginning rather than ending. My hopes, often leveled by the time winter arrived, lifted in autumn.

I also remember a girl, Ethel, about sixteen or seventeen, one of the older girls. Ethel was from the South where some people, I have been told, bathed less often, sometimes once a week. I do not know if that is true, but it was more than just that. Ethel was uncomfortable with changes in her body, tried to ignore them, hiding them when she could not. Perhaps as a result, she avoided bathing unless a housemother insisted.

Another girl, Helen, eighteen and due to graduate from the orphanage, called Ethel "the wall of smell." When someone looked at her, Helen added, "That girl smells nasty."

Said quietly, where Ethel could not hear it, it was funny at first. Funny, until Helen passed it on to some of the boys who were not so quiet about it. I think all that it did was to push Ethel farther into herself. It made me sad because, other than her body odor, she seemed a nice person. It was a lesson for me when it came to rumormongering I never forgot.

Recalling the photograph however, jumped me from autumn to winter, again. I could see our side of the picture. More, I could feel it, feel that wind coming at you like the jaws of a hungry animal. That is my clearest memory of winter at the orphanage – biting wind. I begin to shudder at the thought of it. To get anywhere at The Howard, you had to go out and take the wind head on. Or rather, head down. Head up? It would slash at your face, burning it with stinging ice crystals that stuck to tender skin.

Everything was so spread at The Howard, to get anywhere you had to walk a distance in that wind.

I would guess it was a quarter of a mile from the cottages to the barns, maybe longer. You entered that wind as if stepping into a mad whirlpool, and battled it all the way. There was nothing between the cottages and the few trees along Indian Head Road, winding through the orphanage. Nothing to blunt that savage wind.

"Savage" may be too soft a word to describe it. Even if you were merely slipping from one cottage to the next, you arrived bone-chilled. And you could not hurry. You did, you risked falling on the ice-crusted, hard-as-concrete snow.

It was worse for the older boys since many of their chores took place at the barns. I did not complain much – well, not too much – but never where a boy might hear me.

I talked to myself before leaving our cottage, working up gumption to do what had to be done.

"Don't think about it, Wilhelmina, just do it. Get along now. Pretend it's a July day, the kind that puts you in a daze as you move through it. One step at a time. Think only about that next step. Don't look up and see how much farther it is. And don't look back to see how little you've traveled. Get humming," I would think. You would never sing. Open your mouth to sing and your teeth would flare with pain. "Get humming." I would try to time the melody to my footsteps, like a march. Thoughts like that.

The words, landing on my ears, made me think of war, or preparing myself for battle. I had to rise up to the coming turmoil. I knew the wind was going to push me every which way but where I needed to go. Once again, I wondered why the wind most often came from the front rather than the rear. I would have imagined it would be half and half.

In most mind-over-matter decisions, I believe I do pretty well. I can talk to myself, make up my mind, settle in and do what has to be done. No fretting, no complaining, no dallying. All they do is waste time and energy. As a mother with five children, I cannot afford waste of any kind. But back then, I struggled. Sometimes, I dithered as if I had a choice when in reality, I did not.

I remember trying to get out that door in the morning. "Wilhelmina," I would say, "you can leave now or two minutes from now, but you are leaving. They will close the dining hall. School will not wait. A housemother will get after you." Something like that. "So just get going right now." It worked, just enough to get me moving. I would tighten the scarf across my face, duck my head and stagger out into the wind.

Once, I found myself walking with Ethel, both of us with one shoulder tilted into the wind. In the middle of a gust that chapped lips and stung teeth, she said, "Someday, gonna live in Florida. No more wind, no more snow. Have me my own orange tree. Just sit in the sun and suck on an orange whenever I feel like it."

She turned her face into the wind and hollered, "That's right!"

Ethel was from South Carolina, which was supposed to be warm like Florida, but she never talked of returning. There were rumors about that, too, but I do not care to spread them any farther. Let it be enough for me to say that if the rumors were true, she had her reasons. *Good* reasons.

In the late afternoon, the wind would slacken. The cold air became bearable. After school and training were finished, some of us might wander over to the barns. With all the animals giving off heat, it was actually warm in there, or seemed so.

For city kids like John Henry and me, it was all new. There were horses in Brooklyn, but this was really our first time close to huge animals. We tended to adopt one or another as a pet. Most of them accepted our petting, seemed to respond to our cooing words. We spoke to them as we might a baby.

To the older Southern kids, the animals were "livestock." They seemed less inclined to adopt a pet. I imagined they had seen how it all could end, and held back. For the rest of us, it was a chance to give affection and feel you received it in return.

My favorite was one of the older horses, Scott. "The Prince of the Stable" loved to be brushed. As long as I did not interfere with a chore, I had permission to brush him. When he saw me reach for the brush, he moved to the stall rail so I could reach him. Feelings of love would wash slowly through me, the current warming me further as I brushed. I needed that at the time, needed to express it and feel that it was returned. Thank you, Scott, wherever you may be.

In Brooklyn, there was always a dog here, a cat there, and horses on the streets. But pets were a luxury for the few able to feed them. So many children dreamed of having a pet purses would not allow.

Returning to the cottages, the wind would quiet, gathering force for another bone-rattling night blow. One of the boys, usually Percy or Albert, would start throwing snowballs. They were 13, on that fence between childhood and something different, just before they landed on the "different" side.

Within seconds, we would all join in, the air speckled with smudges of white. It was as if a flock of wild, white birds was swooping and soaring over The Howard skies. Even as I write, I find myself smiling at the memory, as if it just happened.

As close at it seems, *more* as it feels, I am glad I cannot go back to it. No matter the good, it was a time of separation. Now is a time of togetherness, a time of love. I do not have to stagger through frigid air to find and bestow love in a barn. I can simply look up from what I am doing and hear it murmuring in the next room. At any moment, I might feel its arms reach around and embrace me from behind. It is the future I once dreamed of, what I now have.

Chapter Twenty-Six: A World in a Glance

Have you ever noticed someone say something or do something that tells you something about him? Something so much *him*, that nothing needs to be added? Nothing could tell you more clearly. In fact, nothing could tell you more. In that gesture, those words, you not only feel you know something of that person, but something about the whole world. A world in a glance.

You see the gesture and learn something so vital, you feel as if you know who he is. You know instantly whether you want to draw closer or keep a safe distance, even pull away. Someone stoops to pick up a piece of trash in a public place. Says "is not" instead of "ain't." Puts out a bird feeder in winter. Keeps an eye on a frail neighbor, no relation. Well, other than human.

There is nothing in it for the person but the act itself. It is as if, without knowing it, he said, "This is who I am."

I believe most noble things in this world – courage, generosity, caring, what I call the true signs – happen that way. Not by a plan, it was in someone to do that. When the time called for it, called forth what lay within, out it came.

My husband set the wheels in motion about all of this. He told me there are things I do, the way I do them, he would recognize me anywhere. In shadow, he would still know me "from ten others, a hundred, even."

I was curious, no doubt about it. At that moment, he had me. I just had to know, and asked for an example. I knew he had been thinking about it because he was ready. I must admit, I was on tenterhooks.

He spoke of my habit, when we are all out in public, to glance over my right shoulder. Our son, Dukie, will be walking beside me, Catherine and Dorothy just behind, holding Irene's hands. My husband, calling himself the "caboose," will follow with Thelma in his arms. He said I do that to make sure all of my "chicks" are there, beside me or following. Everyone accounted for. Said he sees a "peacefulness" in my face in the certainty of what it sees.

I just cannot say it exactly in his words without sounding immodest. But his words warmed me like the teaspoonful of laudanum a doctor once gave me to quiet a stomachache. I wanted to drift in them – the words – for just a little while.

He spoke of the smile "camped" on my face. I know I smile easily and often, but he called it my "signature." Said when I smile, it is as much me as my name on a piece of paper. He added that "it takes much to erase it." Reminded me that every now and then, unintentionally, he might say something and the smile temporarily vanishes. Said he regrets it deeply when that happens.

His words set off all kinds of feelings, like the bells of many churches tolling on Sunday. Which one do I attend to? I blushed so hard, it was a while before I could sort out what I had just heard. In truth, I was in no hurry. It was all I could do not to ask for another example.

Later, he mentioned that my backward glances come without words. Said they were "unnecessary." He liked that.

He said, "When you peek at us like that, we know what's going on."

Enough about me. I was speaking of the sign that tells you what you need to know about a person. Who he is. *She* is. What you see today, will be there tomorrow.

Just for a second, I want to talk about my son, Dukie. I see him so clearly, not towering (none of us do), but solidly rooted to the Earth. Like a stump, you have to go around him. And he will look you in the eye as you do it, maybe even smile. There is nothing mean about it, it is just him. I mentioned he is the namesake of my father-in-law, the Reverend John W. Hamlin. I see many of the grandfather's good qualities in my son without the unbending stiffness.

The sign that says all. You notice it in the eye-flit of a liar, in the desperately rapid speech of a door-to-door salesman. I find it in the unmade-up face of a woman who welcomes each day as a gift. Anyone with eyes and heart open could see it in a picture of my father-in-law. The set to his face, his eyes, his entire being radiates stern self-control and light. It suggests conviction. (Dukie would not argue with that.) It suggests he is open to the world, that he believes he can manage whatever it brings. Somehow you just know he is what he appears to be, and you can safely confide in him. That if you ask him for an opinion, you will receive it. Do not want it? Then do not ask.

One could say he was posing, that it was as artificial as the light surrounding him. Of course he was posing. That is what you do for a photograph, what the photographer asks of you. And it is likely that the photographic process affected the picture. But how do you create a new person, no matter how hard you try to present a different you? In a painting, yes. The artist can brush away wrinkles and those extra pounds, maybe add an heroic chin. Make you look as you wish to believe you look. But a photograph? For better or worse, that is *you* at that moment, ready or not.

I guess it really does not matter, the cause of Reverend Hamlin's aura. It is what shines through for me. I do believe he gives off a light that contributed to the way his photograph developed. How many photographs have I seen that are flat, frozen with dulled expressions? Lifeless. Then, I look at the photo of my father-in-law. For me, there is no longer a question. His being quivers with gravity, sweep and life, as if it could lift from the page. Somehow, he manages to be firm – I would say *very* firm – but not foreboding, his face a promise.

My husband has told me I "give off light." Here I go again, but he did say that. I might go, "Oh, you," something like that when I am embarrassed, but I love hearing it.

He has also told me I am a "giver," maybe the finest compliment I have ever received. He said he could see it in me from "the moment I first laid eyes on you." It was probably in church, but I am not positive about that. He claimed he saw light when I smiled. Again, I loved hearing this, but had he said that then, I would have been on guard.

Sometimes, John will say to me, "Why are you looking at me like that?"

And I will repeat, "Like that? Like -?"

I am not pretending ignorance. I want him to tell me exactly what he means. I do not like to guess when important words are exchanged and the precise meaning is fogged over. What if you guessed wrong?

He will say, "That look you get."

Again, I will wait.

He will add, "Like you know something I should know."

I will say something like, "Is that my look or your mind?"

He will grin and say, "Your look is in there somewhere. I don't feel like this without those eyes on me."

Usually, one of us starts laughing, the other joining in.

Once in a while, John will say, "Stop looking at me like that. I get it."

Back to light. I believe some people emit light and some absorb it. Some give, some take. Some give more than they take and some take more than they give. I imagine most are in-between, taking some when they are in need, giving when they see it needed. But there are those – not many, fortunately – who only take.

I do not like pointing fingers, but too often it feels like landlords take more than they give. They want the rent on time, no excuses (and no mercy). Yet if something breaks down, they can be awfully slow getting to the problem. The furnace goes out, a faucet springs a leak, a window pane cracks from the cold, good luck!

I have heard it said, more than once, that landlords do not like renting to colored people. As the story usually goes, *we* "let the place run down." It seems most often, by the time we get to a place, it is already run down.

But watch what happens when a colored tenant goes out of his way to fix-up a place? The landlord loves it, decides *his* place is worth more, and raises the rent, forcing the renter out. The new tenant enjoys the hard work of the previous resident, and the landlord takes the credit. I have *seen* landlords advertise the improvements.

There is a balance we must seek between doing just enough and not doing too much. It is a difficult way to live, like perching on a cliff.

Where is the light now? Light is not what I am feeling. More like cooling embers. Better blow a little air on them.

Chapter Twenty-Seven: Damaged by
Something You Cannot Touch

This one is for me. In the past, I have skirted how race has *touched* my life, but this is more than a touch. No Miss Primrose, this time. I am going right at it. Call it what you will, I want to "talk" about something I almost never mention in public. Racialism. Racialism in America.

It is impossible for me to believe there is a colored person in America who has not thought about it. Most likely, thought about it many times. How could we not? It plays a part in our lives every day. Where we live. Where we can go. What we are allowed to do. How we can talk to people. How we can represent ourselves. How we feel about ourselves. How our insides churn at the possibility that we are one suspicious look from being judged unworthy.

If you are hated because of something you have no control over, how can that not *color* your thinking? How can that not affect your expectations, your hopes? How can you not end up damaged by something you cannot touch yet is always there? Even when it may not be, you still feel as if it is. It is always just one cocked eye, one cleared throat, one whispered disapproval away.

In Macy's, I might be fingering a dress, testing how the material would wear against my skin. Over my shoulder, the presence that has been shadowing me finally speaks.

"Ahem! May I help you?"

"No, ma'am," I say. "I'm just looking. But thank you."

The shadow remains. It speaks again.

"Perhaps if you tell me what you're looking for, I can help you find it."

And get me out of the store faster, I think.

I want to say, "If I knew exactly, I would have found it and be gone, wouldn't I?"

But the last thing I ever want to do is create a scene. With all we hold back, if we even let out a trickle, a thunderous flood might follow.

"Thank you, again," I say to the shadow.

I fear that if I turn to face her, one of two things might happen. She will view me as a threat, and use that as an excuse to call security. That or the dam inside me might break, releasing the flood. In which case, she calls security.

"If something strikes me, I will let you know, thank you," I manage to push out slowly. *Very* slowly.

As I knew it would, the shadow continues to move with me. It wears a forceful floral scent – gardenia, maybe – that continues to move when the shadow stops. It speaks once more, the voice a little tighter, the tone assuming that condescension I knew was coming. It always does, eventually.

"Perhaps, we don't have the style you're seeking," it says. "Something I'm sure you can find elsewhere."

As in *anywhere else*. I think, my style? How do you know what my *style* is? Of course, the voice suggests it does know, and it will not be found in Macy's.

And so on. I have been through this before. Not often, but once is enough, forever. Whether I find something I like and can afford it no longer matters. The experience has been *colored* with a darker shade, my mood purple edging to funeral black.

The shadow was, of course, white. Sight unseen, I knew that by the tone and pitch of the voice. It is amazing how much we can communicate by the slant of the voice. Add a tilt to the face, maybe a curled eyebrow, and you might fill an encyclopedia.

Racialism is not the property of one race, religion, or any other group. It can infect anyone. Colored people struggle with it. How can we not? Enslaved for hundreds of years, it is painful for us to admit that it affects us as well. But in America, if it can seep through us, it can pour from white people like a wild river. It can lead them to do things in groups that a single person would recoil from.

In my school history lessons, it struck me that white people have been sorting themselves out from others, forever. In the sorting, they decided they were superior. Okay. I could live with that. How do you challenge something that has little to do with facts, and everything to do with feelings? But in the sorting, whites dishonored what was different. Made it possible to classify the colored races of the world not just as different, but as inferior. Classifying them as less than human, fit to be colonized, converted, and misused.

Why did they do that? I am not speaking of

the horrors that followed – by far the worst, slavery. They stand alone, speaking for themselves, needing no explanation. I am merely asking the question: Why did they do that? No one invited them to. Who invites someone into their house to help themselves to their possessions, to take everything?

I suspect that once you convince yourself another's humanity is questionable, the math changes. Morality is no longer part of the equation. $1 + ? = $ less than 2. More likely, ignore the fraction, and just round it off. $1 + other = 1$.

We kill all other living things for whatever reason moves us – food, clothing, sport, *no* reason. As long as we declare it is our right, we are okay to go ahead.

In America, racial hatred mostly lies quiet and sometimes flares, but it never stops breathing. Nick it, and it can breathe fiercely. Awakened, it can breathe fire, consuming anything, including lives. After years of quiet, the Ku Klux Klan is on the rise again.

A year after The Great War, race riots broke out across the country – Chicago, Washington, Omaha among the worst. People died, hundreds of human beings, most of them colored. We still probably do not know how many. Their communities were destroyed, homes, stores, even churches were burned – on occasion with people inside. Afterward, newspapers offered opinions as to the causes. To me, they were guessing.

One possibility stood tall in the shadows of all that guesswork, hardly mentioned. It was as if newspapers were afraid to mention it, unable to face what it could mean. Thousands of colored men had served in France during the war. When they returned, things were not going to be as they had been. There was no longer a "normal." No matter what the papers said, that had to be part of what those riots were about.

Sadly, my sense is that too many people in America do not seem to want to learn. Yes, I am talking about white people. They seem to turn away from the chance to know about other people, places, something new. *Anything.* If it is different, they are uncomfortable with it, against it, ready to tear it down. At the least bit of upset, look out!

To me, something new or different presents an opportunity. Sometimes it is wonderful, on occasion hard, but always a chance to test ourselves, to learn something. For me, it seems anytime I learn something new, I learn something about myself.

When something different appears, rather than stepping forward to welcome it, many whites seem to step to the side. Like a bullfighter, they let it slide past. Or with contempt, they turn their backs to it. Sometimes, as they avoid what is different, they stick it with something to hurt it.

They call this "tradition." Bad behavior is excused by saying, "This is the way things have always been done."

When things tighten for them, when worry turns to fear, they become angry, and step backwards. And as they step to the past, they finger-point at all that is different. In the end, it seems they blame all but themselves. If there is a means to explain their fear, it is buried under all that anger.

Too often, they are goaded to this destructive thinking by the wealthy and those who serve them. The few people that have so much, want more. In that desire for more, they seem unable or unwilling to stop themselves. And they are not about to allow anything to interfere with what they want.

I know, I was speaking of racialism, and now I am referring to the wealthy. But I believe they are as entwined as the root system that explains a tree. At *its* roots, slavery was always about money.

There is a business aspect to racialism, too. I have heard some of the church elders refer to it as "the system." I know that is only one way of looking at it. But for me it glares like the burning white sun at high noon on a cloudless day. Again, slavery speaks for itself. What could I possibly add to something that has stained this planet?

It strikes me that the wealthy treat the world as a checkerboard. I started to say "chessboard," but their game is simpler. The game continues, jumping over others, until they take everything.

In chess, you win, line-up the fallen pieces after "checkmate," and go again. Often, many of the pieces are still standing as a "gentleman's" agreement and a handshake end it. But in checkers, you continue until there is nothing left. At least in the board game of checkers, you give back the pieces.

The wealthy might build a library or a museum when they are old. But I believe that is a monument to purchase forgiveness and a pathway to Heaven. No, it is a checkerboard way of thinking, the devastation already recorded. The Great War? The war ended, the dead could not be counted, and the wealthy were wealthier. No one could do that math, not even Einstein.

Okay, I said I was going to say it, and I have said it. Whew! Now, climbing down from this soapbox, I just hope I do not fall off and break a leg.

Chapter Twenty-Eight: A Life in the Day

My days pass swiftly, looping by like starlings in flight. With all the work that comes with a family, each day is here and gone. A flash of light and an echo.

At times, I will wonder – but not for long – what all I did today. What did I accomplish? I say often, think it even more, that I love my life. Yet sometimes I can barely recall what passed in a given day. Most days, I am too tired to waste time recalling all that I did, even if I wanted to. Come bedtime, my thoughts are already turning to what lies ahead of me tomorrow. With children, thinking ahead is a must. I cannot coast into a day or time will leave me behind.

I decided for one day, I would jot down everything that happened – what I did, my thoughts, my feelings. Everything.

I picked a weekday, one of those days of unbroken tasks this past summer. My thought – an examined weekday would come closer to telling me what I wished to know. I chose a Wednesday. Mondays and Tuesdays are so consumed with washing and ironing, the details I wished to know might vanish. Wednesday seemed about right, the middle of the week, the middle of everything.

I awoke as almost always, before the children and after my husband left for the Post Office. John leaves in the middle of the night to sort the mail for the carriers later that morning. We agreed it is too early for me to rise, and still have energy for the children's needs through the day.

Pulled on my tired bathrobe, there like a faithful friend, and washed my face in the bathroom sink. From the basement, I lugged a full coal scuttle upstairs to the kitchen, and lit the stove. John will usually do it, but sometimes he does not have the time. More likely, still half-asleep, he forgets.

I found myself humming, "Oh How I Hate To Get up in The Morning." That is not true, but I love the tempo. It sets my motor running like a crank on a car.

I sat at the kitchen table, and gazed out the dew-misted window. Took the first of several quiet moments I treasure each day. If I gazed up, I could see the sky, as blue as a newborn's eye. The alley between our building and the one behind remained dawn dark.

I found myself thinking of falling in love, how it happened between John and me. Before I met him, I had managed to keep away from the drugstore cowboys with their crude lines. You could find them slouching on almost any street corner where there was a candy store.

"I'm goofy about you, baby" or "You're looking swell today, mama." *That*, when I was fourteen, fifteen, sixteen. Good thing I already had a strong sense of what I wanted and what I did not want. They and all their racy talk were not it.

Love for me was always important. Loving someone brought out the best in me. It helped me feel good about the world, hopeful, no matter where I was. By the time I was sixteen, maybe earlier, I knew what I wanted in a husband. He had to be someone who wanted what I wanted, a life built around a family. Someone with his feet on the ground and his eyes straight ahead, not lost in the clouds. And definitely not traveling up and down other women as he was talking to me. I found that in John Francis Hamlin.

After nine years of marriage, I am still in love with him. But now, it is more than that, way more. To put it as simply as I can, I love him. That may sound as if I just repeated myself, but I do not believe so.

Being in love with someone and loving that person are not the same thing, not nearly. The first comes early, and roars up through you like a volcano. But volcanoes can quickly sputter out, or at least quiet down. When they do, what is left behind can appear barren, a gray ashy world left behind. You doubt what you thought you had. But if you remain patient, what seems disappointing, slowly begins to green up into something that can last.

In the end, loving someone is so much more than just being in love with him. You do not want to lose that early fire. But if you wish it to last, it must be banked and fed steadily.

Here I am at twenty-six, writing my thoughts like a recipe. But it is how I feel.

My quiet moment, like a leaf gliding to earth, ended with hungry children wandering into the kitchen for breakfast. The youngest appeared first, the older following.

Breakfast is usually oatmeal. Maybe once a

week, I will work in an egg or pancakes. I tend to stay away from the cereal that comes in boxes. I have nothing against Mr. Kellogg's cornflakes, but I feel better when I prepare the food. I played one-handed patty-cake with Irene (she used two) while I fed Thelma.

Then the real work of the day began. Dishes done, I washed the faces and hands of the younger children, making sure the older did the same. The same with teeth-brushing, I turned it into a game with Irene and Thelma.

"Let's see who can get them the whitest."

I had to help them both, yet the contest led them to want to do it themselves.

"Oh, looks like we have a tie."

"You always say that, Mama," Irene said.

Dressing is followed by hair-brushing and barrette-clipping, rubber bands when I do not have enough clips. Through it all, little arms and legs are going one way and my hands, the other.

Children squared away and the kitchen cleaned up, I moved to a second quiet moment, my bath. While Catherine hop-scotched by the front stoop, Dorothy played with Irene and Thelma inside.

John (when he is around) and Catherine will help when I need it. But Dorothy's closeness to the two youngest allows me time to bathe and dress myself without racing. She understands that the second I am done, she is free to play as she wishes. As it is, she often remains close anyway, hip-connected to Thelma.

I was rinsing my hair when racial images shimmered before my eyes like the new moving pictures. Washing my hands or hair especially, here they come, thoughts so worn they appeared frayed at the edges.

I look at my palms. Place them next to a white person's and try to tell which belongs to whom. My hair? I am the daughter of a colored man and a white woman, my hair the gift of both. Left alone, it tends toward curled length. I have heard colored people refer to it as "good hair." My skin? I would "*pass* the brown-bag test." Heard that, too.

I do not like to think about any of this. These unwelcome thoughts elbow their way in like somebody breaking into a line. More like a policeman without a warrant. I put up with them until they leave. I do not like to think about skin shadings, especially when I think how it has separated people of color.

Did it start with us, or was it originally the workings of white people? I suspect the latter. Did whites trust colored people who tinted closer to them? Were they allowing misbegotten children closer to a cruel hope for naught? Was it a way to turn slave emotions away from the "master" and toward each other? One more means to control?

I caught myself humming "Dixie Land" at the end of that daisy-chain of thoughts. Can you believe that? It was a song of the old South we used to sing at fund-raising concerts for The Howard. I immediately switched to "Lift Every Voice and Sing." When I realized I was brushing tears from my eyes, I switched again, this time to "Bill Bailey." Anything, to snap out of the fog-like sadness reaching for me, and get on with my day.

But this is how it is with daydreams, thoughts flowing like an eternal river. Sometimes they drift slowly, sometimes they can boil up in a flash. You do not give yourself to them so much as they take you where they will.

I finished the preparation I give myself with a quick, last-second mirror check. Caring for my appearance is a means for remaining in control of my life. (I tell myself it is not out of vanity, but I suspect it is that, too.) If you let yourself get out of hand, there is no telling what might follow. Whatever it is, it likely will not be good. It invites giving up, something I will never do.

A quick "Atta-girl" to the mirror, and I was on my way to relieve Dorothy.

Since it was not a wash or ironing day, my morning was focused on the house – cleaning, dusting, sweeping. Beating rugs on the clothesline. I use an old tennis racquet John found sticking out of a trash bin. Better than a broom. A well-placed nail restored its cracked handle.

Through it all, I hum. I might be singing, but if not, I hum. I will start out practicing one of our church-choir hymns. Before I can stop it, I slip into a popular song. Maybe a ragtime melody, it is usually a toe-tapping air that lofts my spirit even higher. For some reason, I feel sneaky when I catch the change, and end up laughing.

I love music, no matter the form. I dream of getting a Victrola someday, and filling my home with music. John speaks of getting a radio, but I tilt toward the Victrola. Right now, we cannot afford either.

I do not need a clock or a church bell to know

when it is noon. Like birds at a feeder you just filled, my children mysteriously reappear at the kitchen, ready for lunch.

My son, Dukie, who was with us this day, set the table. I had made potato salad the night before and lemonade after breakfast, so this meal was easy to prepare. I set hotdogs cooking on the stove and pulled the potato salad from the ice box. I then chipped some ice from the block into their glasses, mine, too. On a warm summer day, there is nothing better than an icy glass of lemonade.

Lunch disappeared as if on one in-breath, the children ready to go once more. Since Dukie set the table, Catherine and Dorothy helped me do the dishes and clean-up the kitchen.

The children playing again, I sat down and put a list together to run to the store for dinner. I had decided to splurge, just a tiny bit, on some lamb chops. My husband loves them. He was raised in Virginia, and still has a taste for "pig meat" and lamb. I thought I might break down and buy a loaf of bread, though usually I bake it. Learned that at The Howard, too.

As I completed the short list, briefly wrapped in silence, I drifted once more. I found myself once again thinking about my life, about who I am. It is something that comes over me like a duty now and then, like cleaning out a closet. It was triggered by that decision, whether to allow myself to buy a loaf of bread or not. Sounds funny when I think about it now, almost pitiful.

Here I am at 26, a counter of pennies. Is that who I am? At the moment it is. And it is indeed a dreary part of life. It can scrape happiness to the bone. You cannot let it rule you. Yet, there it is, turning every day into a contest.

Of course, I am a daughter, a wife, a mother, a church member. I am also a sister, was and always will be. I treasure each. But what am I if you put all of those parts together? I would like to believe I am a *humanitarian*, someone who has feelings and concerns for all people. I like the word, like its sound, what it means to me. But the word is always used with rich and famous people, like Bernard Baruch, who do great deeds. So maybe I cannot say that about myself.

I can safely say the "human" part is in me. *Is* me. But nice as that sounds, it does not satisfy my self-wonderings, the wanderings of my mind. For certain, it is in me to want to help others. I have always been tender-hearted, a strength that has brought out the better in me. I do care, and that is a fact.

Perhaps who I am will be revealed by who I was when I leave this Earth. After I am gone, if one person feels love when she thinks of me, then *that* is who I am.

In the early afternoon, I walked to the store with the girls. More than four months pregnant, I moved a bit slower than usual, unable to carry Thelma any distance. Dukie would have helped, but he had to get back to my in-laws after lunch. They keep a sharp eye on him. *Very* sharp. I would not want to do anything that might cause them distress or a problem for my son. Catherine (six) and Dorothy (five) switched off carrying two-year-old Thelma and holding four-year-old Irene's hand. I always have at least someone holding my free hand, another gripping my skirt. It is a rule – we do everything together, move as one.

People often smile when they see us pass. "Mama hen and all her chicks," one sweet woman said.

Once a week, when I can, I buy them ice cream cones – another reason I count pennies. Okay, and nickels, too. I probably sound like a penny-pincher. I do not like the sound of that expression. It sounds as if someone is stingy. But if penny-pinching can mean being thrifty, then I am a penny-pincher. Whatever one wishes to call it, in my life it is necessary.

On occasion, I get stuck on something like "penny-pincher." It gets me thinking about what I believe, how others might see it, and where the truth lies. I am not comfortable around immodesty in others so I want to make certain I avoid it if possible. That stands at the heart of why I question myself.

Sometimes, it can take me into a whirlpool of wondering. Deep thought and the need not to go too deep spin together. For a woman, especially a colored woman, this is fundamental. Go too deep in public, you could lose something – a job, a patron, your place in *the* line.

John returned mid to late afternoon from the Post Office, and immediately needed to rest. On his feet the entire day, he gets home early because he starts *so* early. I usually have the girls play in another room or outside for a little while. That is unless he asks for them, which he frequently does.

187

I brought him a glass of iced lemonade and mentioned an opportunity to go out Saturday night. We love to dance and listen to music. My mother had offered to babysit. He was for it.

"Are you up for the one-step?" I said, what some call the "fox trot."

"Right now," he said, laughing, "I am ready for the no-step. But I could listen to some jazz. Come Saturday night, I'll be there."

Later in the afternoon, while John and I chatted, Dorothy helped me wax furniture. When I rose to prepare dinner, John went searching for the can of "3 in 1." Finding it, he began to oil the stiff, squeaky door hinges and window latches throughout our apartment.

From a window, I called the children in to "wash up" for dinner. I fried the lamb chops, the way John likes them, served them with mashed potatoes and lima beans. He calls them "butter beans." I would prefer to broil the chops, but he has that taste for Southern cooking. One of the chops I cut into tiny pieces for Irene and Thelma.

John still laughs about me calling the evening meal "dinner." Where he grew up, "dinner" was the midday meal.

After dinner, October daylight fading, I let the children play out in front, close to the building's steps. While I cleaned up, John read *The New York Evening Journal*, an afternoon paper for evening reading. Before anything else, he will check to see if Babe Ruth hit any home runs that afternoon. When he gets to the news, he will read me the bits and pieces he wants to share. I appreciate that. Though I read the paper when I can, often I just do not have the time or energy. But if something horrible has happened, he will not mention it to me. I learned of the "anarchist" bombings and the Sacco and Vanzetti trial despite his efforts to protect me. I think he tried to hide the paper when they started sterilizing all those women, colored included. I know he has done that whenever the horror of racialism makes the paper.

Paper read, he set about polishing shoes for everyone until I finished up in the kitchen. Tomorrow, I will check with my mother to reconfirm Saturday night. It is just a quick walk to her apartment, and even if we could afford a telephone, she could not.

She already said, "I'll be there, lass," but I want to be sure. Nights out do not come often.

At twilight, violet clouds rolling up the darkening blue sky, John and I joined the kids out front. While he chatted with a neighbor, I let myself drift in the purple gloaming, thinking of Saturday night.

There were other things that needed doing. Sewing and darning alone could take an evening and then some. But there will always be something else to do. I decided to relax and flow along with the evening and my thoughts. Even the squawk of a distant radio could not disturb the serenity of my mind. I suspect someday we will have a radio, much as John would like one.

Saturday night holds such promise, a little blessing likely to become a lifetime memory. The change from the everyday helps me so much. I thought how that might sound, the chance for happiness *away from* my children. But it is just different, something that makes the everyday a bit easier. Afterward, I return home uplifted, ready to move forward into the next day, not as mind-tired.

Each of my children is a song sung every day, so I am really never apart from music. The pulse and rhythms of life are just right for me. I am not asking for more (well, more money would be nice), remain thankful for what I have.

But that said, when it comes to music, I enter seventh heaven, just as I did performing at The Howard. Sometimes it is all I can do not to break out in song, accompanying the band without an invitation. When I dance with John, I feel I am on a ship, and the music is the water. It moves us according to its currents. I often feel the same way just sitting and listening, swaying with the rhythm sliding around me.

Street lights, blinking on in the coming darkness, alerted me to the children's bedtime. I excused myself, and headed to start their baths. I do not bathe them every night – the water bill – but everyone washes or is washed at the sink. I make certain they are clean before they get into bed.

I try to make it fun for them, a quick story or magic trick followed by a lullaby. With the two youngest, I will sing down to a hum, like I am dimming a light. With Catherine and Dorothy, I might lie with them for a moment and let them tell *me* a story. The tale is usually thrown together higgledy-piggledy from something that happened that day. Turns out to be a great way to know if anything might be troubling them. Bedtime is not a battle.

The children down, I returned to the front steps where several couples were chatting in the cooling evening. John retired shortly. As I have said, his day starts so early. Cooling but still August warm in October, I sat for a while, not apart from the conversation, but not of it, either. I would "Mm-hm" now and then, out of courtesy. But I was drawn to the sounds of the city settling in for the night. A horse will nicker here, a dog bark there, a cat answering. In the distance, you might hear a horn honk or the baying of a police siren, maybe an ambulance. The sounds eventually thinned, and in the quiet, my day spirit settled as well.

I excused myself once more, and entered our hushed apartment. John and the children asleep, I prepared myself for bed. Night time in the bathroom – yes, the bathroom once again – is the peacefulness I find at day's end.

As I brushed my hair, my thoughts turned to happiness, to what makes me happy. For some people, happiness is fickle, depends on something special happening. It can turn up suddenly, like a carnival man trying to get at money you do not have. And then, like the carnival itself, vanish in the night. For me, happiness seems a part of my nature, mostly just there. Lucky me. As I said, I remain grateful.

But I have also learned that, in the middle of anything, anytime, something can be taken from you. Often, it seems as if there is nothing you can do about it. You learn to live with it, but uneasily, careful your hopes do not run away.

Like a person who has suffered cancer, but is now "okay," never again will that person live easily. Each twinge or ache might be a message that cancer has returned. It has been that way for me since I was first separated from my parents and sent to The Howard. Things happen, and I cannot keep up with them.

I looked at a picture of myself taken when I was maybe twenty-two. Someone said, "Smile!" and I did. But I see something else in the picture, something hard to explain. My eyes appeared focused on something beyond the camera, almost as if I was in a daze. I was doing what I was supposed to, yet I was not totally a part of it. It was as if I was almost happy, but not quite. As if I was there, and yet, not quite. If I was not quite there, where was I?

Odd, a day that began bright with hope, ended on a question. Like something on a frayed clothesline, something you cannot quite pull back. It is something within me that keeps me uncertain. But I can live with that if Providence favors my husband and children. That is my prayer.

Chapter Twenty Nine: Changes

The year I was born (1903), a flying machine with a man aboard flew on the beaches of North Carolina. From the pictures I have seen, it looked like a giant toy, a cat's cradle with wings. One snip, and it all would collapse. And yet, this giant toy, this airplane flew.

Just twelve years later (1915), my last year at The Howard, men were flying airplanes in war. Over France, they were shooting each other down, dropping bombs. To read about it was shocking, but worse, it was absolutely paralyzing to think about. That fragile toy, that cat's cradle stretched over wings, had become a weapon, a machine of death.

Twelve more years, 1927, the year Thelma was born, Charles Lindbergh, "Lucky Lindy," flew across the Atlantic Ocean. Just *two* years ago! In one picture, his airplane, The Spirit of St. Louis, looked like a giant silver bird, something out of a fable. In less than a quarter of a century, that *toy* had carried a man across an ocean.

What in the world is happening? The changes come so fast. I just begin to grasp something, and *poof*, the next day it has changed again. I can barely absorb it all, do not know what to make of it. So much so, sometimes I doubt what my eyes and ears behold.

While I marvel at some of the changes, I also worry about them. Actually, I worry more about me.

Will I be able to keep up with it all? Will the changes leave me behind, lost and unable to explain them to my children? How would I be able to explain something I do not yet understand?

The shock of it all, leaving me frozen with uncertainty, brought back memories of my years at The Howard. I recalled times when what I saw or heard was not what adults tried to convince me of.

At the root of so much of my bewilderment was money. That was one thing that never changed, still has not. $0 + 0 = 0$ or less. Is that a surprise? Not to me. Money – or rather its want – tied people in knots, forcing them to do things that chafed their pride. Horrible as it sounds, it made good people beggars.

Superintendent Gordon, the matron and the housemothers pretended to worship visitors, especially rich white people. Behind Reverend Gordon's smile, you could see the pain lines around his eyes stretch longer, crack wider. It was as if he and the others were on a stage, smiles painted on their faces. They were trying to get those white people they were fussing over to open their hearts. If not, then at least their wallets.

At twelve, and even earlier, *this* I understood. It was all aimed at raising the money we so desperately needed. That was okay. What bothered me? It seemed as if the adults were also asking us to pretend it was not pretend. They think children do not know, but they do. Maybe it was to ease their burden, but it added to mine. It chipped away at the trust in adults I so badly needed to hold on to.

Again, that is what money can do. People,

who need it so desperately, will allow others who have it, shame them for it. I recall one women's club of young to middle-age ladies. They insisted we appear before them so they could tell us what they were going to give. I could tell it made *them* feel good.

Once we began performing – "dancing for our dinner," someone said, laughing – it was okay. But it was not funny. For me, there was something holy about singing, but it was okay. As I have said many times, I loved to sing, would break into song anywhere. Yet, as I approached twelve and felt the first stirrings of womanhood, my mind seemed to change, too. It seemed to grow. I began to see and understand things I could not just a year or two earlier.

An awakening came with the "Colored Spirituals" we sang. These were songs the white audience with the fat wallets and purses wanted. Songs like "Old Black Joe," "Ma Pickaninny Babe," "Rockin in De Win," and of course, "Dixie Land." Here we were performing in Brooklyn, New York, maybe the heart of the North. Yet when we sang "Dixie," sometimes white people would clap, stomp their feet and sing along. Some would stand up and cheer.

There are no *bad* songs. Music is music, free notes strung together like Christmas lights, parts of itself and nothing else. But when I came to know what people made of those songs, what the words stood for? *That* was different. Behind some of those words lay a darkness beyond light. And that was so not good, it was bad.

There we were helping white people pretend. Pretend we were singing about a glorious time that brought smiles to their red mouths and tears to their red eyes. A time they liked to imagine that never was. Some of their people may have died because of those songs and the lies they stirred. In dresses petal-white against brown skin, we sang about slavery, our angelic voices recalling a dream.

It left me feeling uneasy, as if I were singing a lie. In times past, I had never felt awkward about singing. Now, I was mindful of what I was singing, feeling the first rousing of discomfort.

Yet, perhaps clearer than ever, I understood why we were singing songs about slavery. We were, all of us, straining to keep The Howard alive. You played your part, did whatever you had to do – smile, lower your eyes, bend your knee. I did.

I believe this was when I learned that life, for what it gave, made its demands. Sometimes, in return for what it gave, it took something away. This was a hard lesson for me in the end, one I have never forgotten. It was so powerful, I have had to battle in my mind not to become jaded about life. Sometimes, it seems I battle it most every day.

When I started this remembrance, I spoke of laughter, of song, of turning to the sun. These were the benedictions I sought to keep my spirits up when life pressed at me. I still laugh, most definitely sing, and look for sunlight when I can. But sometimes now, I have to remember to do that.

When was the last time you *laughed*, Wilhelmina? What was that *song* you could not get out of your mind last week? The last time you got out in the *sun* was when? Is this what change has wrought? In trying to keep up, have I only fallen farther behind?

Smiles, songs, sun – they have become like one more task I have to work into my busy day. That is not good. I suspect – no, I believe – I am doing them less spontaneously as life takes its toll.

I must keep an eye on this, and not risk losing a good part of who I am. If for no other reason, it would be a loss for my children, as well. I will not let that happen.

Chapter Thirty: The Stirring Within

I was hanging out wash when I felt a fluttering inside. For the first time, I felt the quickening of my baby.

It had to be a Monday. I was sitting on a window sill, running wet clothes on a line that stretched to the building behind us. There are so many lines across the alley, sometimes it looks like a flag celebration.

Busy with a task as usual, I was lost in my thoughts. I was humming "Ave Maria" as an autumn breeze blew across my wet hands. The air smelled of wet cotton and the iodine I had dabbed on a finger cut earlier. I felt myself fill with hope as I always do when the air cools.

There was rain in the wind, smelling like water from a rusty rain barrel, metallic. But the lingering taste of honey on toast from my breakfast battled the bitterness to a standstill.

In the breeze as I worked, my senses were up, swelling like mushrooms after rain. The sun that managed to sneak down the alley landed like tiny explosions against bits of stained glass. Reflected in the windows, pots of geraniums flamed into red fire. I could hear the junkman calling, children shouting and laughing, the screech of elevated steel. I noticed the sound of water flowing in pipes.

I switched to whisper-singing "Alexander's Ragtime Band.

"C'mon along, c'mon along, Alexander's Ragtime Band."

And off I went, my voice welling up through the whisper. I love "Ave Maria," but its beauty can also leave me sad, haunted by something I cannot express. It seems to reach back to a time before I lived. Could that be?

Then came the stirring within. Within seconds, the first steps of life poked at me and all other thought vanished. My senses funneled to the baby inside, as did my thoughts.

I began, as I always have, to wonder how we would manage with the added expense, wondered how I would manage an additional child and the added work. My thoughts spiraled in repeating circles like a runner on an oval, only mine circled backwards

With this wondrous store of good memories, the past is still painful for me. I immediately think of my first child, Dukie, my only son, living with my in-laws. When my husband and I married, we lived with his parents, Reverend John W. and Mrs. Frances Walker Hamlin. The want of money made it so. What else?

Two families under one roof are just that – two families. $1 + 1$ does not equal a bigger 1. This time the math makes sense. $1 + 1 = 2$. No matter the love that exists, it is not easy. Reverend Hamlin is a good man, well-respected within our church community. But he is also a prideful man with his own sense of how things should be done.

When my husband and I managed to afford

an apartment, our son remained with the Hamlins. Again, money made the decision. Memories of my own separation from my parents to The Howard Orphanage made this particularly painful. But with John at the Post Office and me at the wig factory, someone had to care for our son. I was grateful to the Hamlins, and remain so. But I was also tormented without mercy that my first born was being raised by someone else.

Within the next three years, Catherine and then Dorothy came. Still under water financially, we ended up living for a while with my mother, Kate. As a widow with health problems, she was barely able to survive.

This was probably one of the most difficult periods of my life, darkened by the absence of my son. Of course, I saw him from time to time, but that is not the same. Not nearly. Though he was aware of me as his mother, he answered to the Hamlins, no one more than the Reverend.

Call it fate, call it life, call it luck – to this day, our son has never lived with us. It tears at me, at times so unmercifully, I have to battle to remember my gratitude for the help. I accept the reality as financially necessary, but the emotional struggle has no ending. It lingers like a chafed blister that will not heal.

When I think of this, I then think *this* child in me will fit into our lives. Come *hell* or high water! My gosh. I am not comfortable with that word. But I use it, knowing it says how fiercely I feel about this. When I begin to fret over money, I just put my worries in the mental drawer labeled "*Somehow.*"

I wonder at times how many children I am destined to have. The child growing in me will make six. I believe that is enough.

The wondering leads me back to the odd arithmetic that was never in any of my math books. It was so easy for me when one plus one equaled two. I would like to find more of that in life, but I do not.

The beating heart of my life is my children. I do not question that, just as I must accept each child adding to the struggle for daily bread. With poverty a creeping shadow, it adds up to uncertainty. $1 + 1 =$? In this case, you end up all balled up without an answer. Do they cancel each other out? Is it really $1 - 1$ in disguise? Are you back where you started? Not with children of course, but with the means to survive.

I have felt the judgment of tut-tutting eyes on John and me, none more powerful than my father-in-law's. The eyes ask an unspoken question. If you cannot afford them, why do you keep having them? I know, and I do not know. I know they are born of love, and received with love. And gratitude. But I do not know how to answer the same question.

People say, "The Lord will provide," my father-in-law among them. If so, why do so many of them look sideways at us when we have another child? Do you stop loving? How do you do that? I do not think that is an answer.

I think ordinarily $5 + 1 = 6$. But when I look at my children before me, 5 becomes 4, and here I go again. So, is it $5 - 1 = 4 + 1 = 5$? In my mind, it is still six. Or soon will be.

Somewhere in my math schooling, I

remember a symbol for "infinity." A symbol for something so unknowable, it cannot be counted. It looked like an 8 lying on its side, as if it toppled from the weight of its meaning.

Is my question really, "how much is $1 + \infty$?" Put that way, the answer would appear to be "never to be known." Am I never to be allowed an answer? Or is the answer given at the end of life? Perhaps the answers to the puzzle of life come to light only after the last piece is fitted in.

Maybe I think about infinity more than I realize, about things that cannot be answered easily. Maybe that is what produces the crazy math, thoughts about things only a life can answer. Or God.

Yet, overriding everything, every concern, worry, fret, is the blossoming love for the coming child that floats within me. Once you feel it moving, all of the "what ifs" and "maybes" disappear.

Afterword

On April 10, 1930, Wilhelmina Johnson Hamlin died of complications just days after giving birth to her sixth child and namesake, Wilhelmina ("Shing"). She was twenty-six-years-old.

Her loss appeared to have left her husband and six children able to speak of her thereafter only with throat-constricting difficulty, if at all.

Wilhelmina's husband, John F. Hamlin, managed with great determination, and the help of his sister Gertrude and her husband, as well as his second wife, Helen, to raise the children as an intact family.

In the early twenty-first century, more than seventy years after Wilhelmina's death, an attempt was made to interview her daughter, Dorothy Hamlin Rhodes, as part of a historical preservation effort. In the middle of the recording, when asked about her mother, Dorothy – six years old when Wilhelmina died – broke down.

According to her daughters, Linda Rhodes Jones and Wilhelmena Rhodes Kelly, Wilhelmina's granddaughters, when Dorothy died in 2010, her final word, repeated several times was "Mama."

Acknowledgements

Three people made this book possible. Without their constancy and unstinting assistance, the story of Wilhelmina Johnson Hamlin would have remained a haunting specter of my imagination. Without their personal troves of photos, annals, remembrances, and encouragement, I would have had little to anchor my imagination to a history-based reality, my intention from the outset.

Linda Rhodes Jones and Wilhelmena Rhodes Kelly allowed me entry into their lives and personal histories as those related to their maternal grandmother, Wilhelmina Johnson Hamlin. They guided me through Weeksville, their grandmother's home neighborhood and the original African-American community now incorporated within the Crown Heights section of Brooklyn. The experience granted me intonations of Wilhelmina's life, invaluable to the imagining.

Leo Ostebo, a former teacher of mine, and the driving force behind the preservation of local history through the Kings Park Heritage Museum, not only provided the original idea, but then unceasingly supported it with all the historical documentation at his disposal. Here he was, fifty years after my high school graduation, exposing me to gaps in my knowledge – still teaching.

For a debt I cannot repay, I can only offer my eternal gratitude. The three of you added an unexpected but cherished chapter to my life.

About the Author

Raised in New York City and King's Park, New York, fiction writer, RJ McCarthy, has lived in the South more than half his life. He received his Ph.D. from the University of South Carolina in 1972 and worked as a Clinical Psychologist before retiring in 2006 to devote himself to writing full-time.

McCarthy is a member of the Virginia Writer's Group, the North Carolina Writer's Network, and both the Franklin County and Vance County Arts Councils. He's been writing fiction for 40 years and has a binder full of rejections to prove it. *Quarry Steps Up*, crime fiction, was his first published novel. Married and the father of two adult children, he and his wife, Susan, reside with two dogs and three cats in Henderson, North Carolina. Visit the author's website: rjmccarthybooks.com